Riven Bonds

A Novel

Vol. I

by

E. Werner

Double 9 BOOKS

Riven Bonds

A Novel

Vol. I

by E. Werner

ISBN: 978-93-71810-21-0

Published by

DOUBLE 9 BOOKS

2/13-B, Ansari Road
Daryaganj, New Delhi – 110002
info@double9books.com
www.double9books.com
Tel. 011-40042856

ABOUT THE AUTHOR

Elisabeth Bürstenbinder, born on November 25, 1838, in Berlin, Germany, was the daughter of a well-established family whose intellectual and cultural influences shaped her literary direction. Writing under the pseudonym Ernst Werner, she became a prominent figure in 19th-century German literature. Her career began to attract attention with the publication of Hermann in 1870, which marked the start of a long and productive writing life. She became known for works that combined emotional depth with moral dilemmas and examined the conflict between personal duty and individual desire. Several of her novels, including Sacred Vows, Fickle Fortune, and Riven Bonds, were translated into English, broadening her reach beyond German-speaking audiences. Her stories often portrayed layered emotional experiences and highlighted the tension between romantic ideals and societal roles. Bürstenbinder's writing was appreciated for its narrative clarity and the ability to balance sentiment with structural discipline. She spent her later years in Merano, Italy, where she died on October 10, 1918, at the age of 79. Her literary contributions reflected a strong narrative voice that engaged with the cultural questions of her time while retaining emotional resonance for a broad readership.

CONTENTS

CHAPTER I

The curtain fell amid thunders of applause from the whole house. Boxes, pit, and gallery unanimously demanded the reappearance of the singer, who, in the finale of the act just concluded, had carried all away with her. The whole audience became excited, and would not be calmed, until, greeted with applause, which broke forth with renewed vigour, overwhelmed with flowers, wreaths, and homage of all kinds, the object of this ovation showed herself, in order to thank the public.

"This is quite like an evening in an Italian theatre," said an elderly gentleman, entering one of the boxes in the first tier. "Signora Biancona seems to understand the art of filling the otherwise quiet and smoothly-flowing patrician blood of our noble Hanseatic town with the fire of her Southern home. The infatuation for her begins to be quite an epidemic. If it continue to increase in this way, we shall see the Exchange voting her a torchlight procession, and the Senate of this free town, appearing before her *in corpore*, to lay their homage at her feet. Were I in your place, Herr Consul, I should make this proposition to both these Corporations. I am sure it would meet with an enthusiastic reception."

The gentleman to whom these words were addressed, and who was sitting by a lady, apparently his wife, in the front of the box, seemed unable to withdraw himself from the universal excitement. He had applauded with an energy and perseverance worthy of a better cause, and turned round now, half-laughing, half-annoyed.

"I was sure of it; the critic must place himself in opposition to the general voice. Certainly, Herr Doctor, in your abominable morning paper, you spare neither Exchange nor Senate; how, then, could Signora Biancona hope to find mercy?"

The Doctor smiled a little maliciously, and drew near to the lady's chair, when a young man, who had been sitting beside her, rose politely to make way for him.

"Herr Almbach," said the lady, introducing them, "Herr Dr. Welding, the editor of our morning paper, whose pen--"

"For Heaven's sake, my dear madam," interrupted Welding, "do not throw discredit on me, at once, in the gentleman's eyes. One has only to be introduced as critic to a young artist, and immediately one gains his deepest antipathy."

"Possibly," laughed the Consul, "but this time your keenness has failed you. Herr Almbach, thank goodness, can never be in a position to come before your judgment seat. He is a merchant."

"Merchant!" a look of astonishment was turned towards the young man, "then I certainly apologise for my mistake. I should have taken you for an artist."

"There, you see, dear Almbach, your forehead and eyes do you a bad turn again," said the Consul, playfully. "What would your people at home say to the exchange? I almost fear they would look upon it as an insult."

"Perhaps. I do not consider it as such," said Almbach, bowing slightly to Welding. The words were intended to carry on the joking tone that was begun, but there lay in them a half-concealed bitterness, which did not escape Dr. Welding. He fixed his eyes searchingly on the young stranger's features; but just at that moment the lady turned towards him, and resumed the interrupted topic.

"You must allow, Herr Doctor, that Biancona was quite ravishing to-night. This young, dawning talent is indeed, a new star in our theatrical firmament."

"Which will some time become a shining sun, if it carry out what to-day it promises. Certainly, dear madam; I do not deny it at all, even although this future sun shows a few spots and imperfections at present, which naturally escape so enthusiastic a public."

"Well then, I advise you not to lay too much stress on these imperfections," said the Consul, pointing to the pit. "There, below, sits an army of knights, infatuated about the Signora. Take care, Herr Doctor, or you will receive at least six challenges."

The malicious smile played round Welding's lips again, as he cast a glance of irony towards young Almbach, who had listened silently, but with darkly lowering brow, to the conversation.

"And perhaps a seventh, also! Herr Almbach, for instance, seems to look upon the opinion which I have just expressed as a species of high treason."

"I regret, sir, to be so much behind you as regards criticism," coolly replied the one addressed. "I--" hereupon his eyes flashed almost passionately, "I am accustomed to worship genius unconditionally."

"A very poetical style of criticism," sneered Welding. "If you were to repeat that in person to our beautiful Signora, and in the same tone, I could promise you her most complete favour. Besides, I am this time in the pleasant position of being able to tell her in the article which will appear to-morrow, that hers is indeed a talent of the first order, that her faults and failings are only those of a beginner, and that it lies in her power to become eventually, a musical celebrity. She is not one at present."

"In the meanwhile, that is praise enough from your lips," said the Consul; "but I think we must retire now; the brilliant part of Biancona is over, the last act offers nothing for her *rôle*, she hardly appears again upon the stage, and our duties as hosts call us to our reception evening. May I offer you a seat in our carriage, Herr Doctor? Your critic's duty is also about at an end; and you, dear Almbach, will you accompany us, or shall you remain to the last?"

The young man had also risen. "If you and your gracious lady will allow it--the opera is new to me--I should like--"

"Very well then, remain without ceremony," interrupted the other in a friendly manner, "but be punctual to-night. We count positively upon your coming."

He gave his arm to his wife, to lead her away. Dr. Welding followed them.

"How could you think," scoffed he, when in the corridor, "that your young guest would move from the spot so long as Biancona had only one more note to sing, or that he would be debarred from helping to form a guard to her carriage with the rest of our gentlemen? The beautiful eyes of the Signora have done much harm already--he has caught fire worse than the others."

"We must hope not," said the lady, with a touch of concern in her voice. "What would his father and mother-in-law, and, above all, his young wife say?"

"Is Herr Almbach married already?" asked Welding, astonished.

"Two years since," replied the Consul. "He is nephew and son-in-law of my business correspondents. The firm is Almbach and Co., not a very important, but a most substantial, respectable house. Besides, you do the young man injustice with your suspicions; at his age one is easily carried away, particularly when, as here, one so seldom enjoys a musical treat. Between ourselves, Almbach has rather middle-class views, and keeps his son-in-law tightly by the head. He will take care that any harm which those eyes could do, shall be kept far from his house. I know him well enough on that point."

"All the better for him," said the Doctor, laconically, as he seated himself by the married pair in the carriage, which took the direction of the harbour, where the palaces of the rich business men were situated.

An hour later, a numerous company was assembled in the merchant's drawing-rooms. Consul Erlau was one of the richest, most influential men in this wealthy commercial town, and even although this circumstance was sufficient to ensure him an undisputed position, he made it, in addition, a point of honour, to hear his house called the most brilliant and hospitable in H----. His reception evenings gathered together every notability which the town had to offer. There was never a celebrity who did not appear several times, and even the star of the present season--*prima donna* Biancona, who was here with the temporary Italian Opera Company, had accepted the invitation which she had received, and appeared after the end of the performance. The young actress, after her evening's triumph in the theatre, was of course the centre of attraction for all the company. Besieged by the gentlemen with every species of homage, overwhelmed with compliments from the ladies, distinguished by the host and his wife with most flattering attentions, she was unable to escape from the stream of admiration which flowed towards her from all sides, and which, perhaps, was due as much to her beauty as her genius.

Both were indeed united here. Even without her highly-worshipped talent, Signora Biancona was not likely ever to be overlooked. She was one of those women, who, wherever they appear, know how to attract, and, oft to a dangerous degree, retain eye and senses; whose entrancing charms do not lie only in their beauty, but far more in the singular, almost witch-like magic, which certain natures exercise, without any one being able to account for its cause.

It seemed as if a breath of the glowing South, full of colour, lay upon this apparition, who, with her dark hair and complexion, her large, deep, black eyes, out of which shone such an ardent, full life, contrasted go strangely with these Northern surroundings. Her manner of speaking and moving was, perhaps livelier, less constrained than the rules of '*convenance*' demanded, but the fire of a Southern nature, which broke forth with every emotion, had an entrancing grace. Her light ethereal-looking costume was not at all conformed to the reigning fashion, but it appeared to be especially invented to display the advantages of her figure in the best light, and held its own triumphantly amongst the more magnificent toilets of the ladies around her.

The Italian was a being who seemed to stand above all the forms and trammels of everyday life, and there was no one in the company who did not willingly accord her this distinction.

Almbach, too, had found his way here after the close of the theatre, but he was quite a stranger to the circle, and evidently remained so, notwithstanding the well-meant attempts of the Consul to make him acquainted with one or another of the guests. All fell through, partly on account of the young man's almost moody silence, partly on account of the gentlemen's manners to whom he was introduced, and who, belonging almost entirely to the circles of the Exchange and Finance, did not think it worth while to take much trouble about the representative of a small firm. He was standing quite isolated at the lower end of the room, looking apparently indifferently at the brilliant crowd, but his eyes always turned to one point, which to-night was the magnet for all the assembled gentlemen.

"Now, Herr Almbach, you make no attempt to approach the circle of the sun of the drawing-room," said Dr. Welding, coming up to him, "shall I introduce you there?"

A slight uncomfortable blush, at his secret wish having been divined, covered the young man's face.

"The Signora is so occupied on all sides that I did not venture to trouble her also."

Welding laughed, "Yes, the gentlemen all seem to follow your method of criticism, and equally to admire genius unconditionally. Well, art has the privilege of inspiring all with enthusiasm. Come, I will present you to the Signora."

They crossed to the other side of the drawing-room where, the young Italian was, but it really gave them some trouble to penetrate the circle of admirers surrounding the honoured guest, and to approach her.

The Doctor undertook the introduction; he named his companion, who, to-day, had for the first time the pleasure of admiring the Signora on the stage, and then left him to set himself at ease in the "sun's circle." This designation was not so badly chosen; there really was something of the scorching glow of this planet, at its midday height, in the glance which she now turned upon Almbach.

"Then you were also in the theatre this evening?" asked the Signora, lightly.

"Yes, Signora."

Tie answer sounded curt and gloomy; no other word, none of those compliments which the actress had heard so plentifully to-day, but the look in the young man's eyes must have made up for his monosyllabic reply. It is true that he only met Signora Biancona's for a moment, but their lighting-up was seen and understood; it said much more than all spoken flatteries.

The other gentlemen might receive no high opinion of the new arrival's social talents; who did not even understand how to make a pretty speech to a lady. They ignored him thoroughly. The conversation, in which the Consul now took part, became more general; they spoke of music, of a known composer and his new work, just now causing great sensation, as to whose conception Signora Biancona and Dr. Welding had a difference of opinion. The former was full of enthusiasm for it, while the latter accorded it very little value. The Signora defended her opinion with Southern vivacity and was supported therein by all the gentlemen, who took her side from the commencement, while the Doctor persisted coolly in his own. The battle grew more determined, until at last the Signora became somewhat annoyed, and turned away from her opponent.

"I regret very much that our Conductor was prevented from accepting to-day's invitation. He plays this composition perfectly, and I fear it requires a performance to enable the company to judge which of us two is right."

The guests were of the same opinion, and regretted the Conductor exceedingly, none offered to replace him. The playing of this music did not appear to keep pace with the very remarkable enthusiasm for it, until Almbach came forward suddenly and said, "I am at your disposal, Signora."

She turned quickly towards him and said with evident appreciation, "You are musical, Signor?"

"If you and the rest of the company will bear with the attempt of an 'amateur,'" he made a gesture of enquiry to the master of the house, and as the latter agreed eagerly, he went to the piano.

The composition under discussion, a modern show-piece in the fullest sense of the word, owed its general popularity less to its real worth--of which it had indeed very little--than to its great difficulty of execution. Even the simple possibility of playing it at all, required a masterly power over the instrument. People were accustomed only to hear it performed by high-standing professionals, and therefore looked half-astonished, half-contemptuously at the young man who volunteered his services with so little concern. He had certainly apologised for being an amateur, but still it was presumptuous to attempt this in Consul Erlau's house, where the playing of so many celebrities had been heard and admired.

The guests were so much the more astonished that Almbach showed himself perfectly equal to all these difficulties, as, without even a note of music before him, he overcame them by playing at once, with an ease and certainty which would have done honour to a regular artist. At the same time he understood to put such fire into his performance as carried away even the older and more expectant hearers. The piece of music under his hands seemed to acquire quite a different form; he gave it a meaning, which no one, perhaps not even the composer himself, had attached to it, and especially the finale, rendered in a somewhat stormy *tempo*, brought him most plenteous applause from all sides.

"Bravo, bravissimo, Herr Almbach!" cried the Consul, who was the first to come up, and who shook him heartily by the hand, "we must really be grateful to the Signora and Doctor, whose musical dispute assisted us to the discovery of such a talent. You modestly announce an attempt, and give us a performance of which the most finished artist need not be ashamed. You have helped our Signora to a brilliant victory; she is right--unconditionally right, and the Doctor this time remains, with his attack, decidedly in the minority."

The singer had also approached the piano.

"I, too, am grateful to you for having responded to my wish in so knightly a manner," she said, smiling; now lowering her voice, "but take care; I fear my critical enemy will still fight with you as to the mode in which you proved my opinion. Was the playing, above all the finale, quite correct?"

A treacherous gleam shot across the young man's countenance, but he also smiled.

"It accorded with your views, and received your applause, Signora--that is enough for me."

"We will speak of it later," whispered the Signora quickly, as now the lady of the house drew near to pay some civilities to her young guest, and the greater part of the company followed her example. A stream of phrases and compliments swept over Almbach, his playing was charming; his execution--where had he studied music? The less he had been noticed before--the less he was known to them, the more he had astonished all by suddenly coming forward, added to the young man's modesty, which hardly permitted him to reply to all the questions addressed to him; every one present felt himself involuntarily to be a sort of Mecænas, and was prepared to give the young genius his complete protection. Was it really modesty that closed Almbach's lips? Sometimes a species of mockery flashed in his eyes, as again and again this exquisite performance was extolled; and it was declared that this composition had never been heard in perfection before. He seized the first opportunity to escape from the attention paid him, and in this attempt was taken possession of by Dr. Welding.

"Is it possible to reach you at last? You are regularly besieged with compliments. Just one word, Herr Almbach; shall we go in here?"

He pointed to an adjoining room, into which both had scarcely entered, before the Doctor continued in a somewhat sharp tone--

"Signora Biancona was right: that is, according to your performance. My attack was directed against the composition as it exists in the original. May I ask where you found this very peculiar arrangement of it? Until this moment it was quite unknown to me."

"How do you mean, Herr Doctor?" asked the young man, coolly. "I only know the piece of music in that form."

Welding looked him up and down, an expression of annoyance struggled with one of undisguised interest in his face, as he replied--

"You appear to gauge the musical knowledge of your audience quite correctly, if you venture to offer them such things. They hear the air, and are contented; but sometimes there are exceptions. For instance, it would interest me very much to know from whom certain variations emanate, which utterly change the character of the whole; and as regards the finale, entirely; was this daring improvisation, perhaps, the attempt of an amateur also?"

Almbach raised his head somewhat defiantly, "And if it were, what should you say to it?"

"That it was a great mistake of your people to make you a merchant."

"Herr Doctor, we are in a merchant's house."

"Certainly," answered Welding, calmly, "and I am the last to depreciate that class, especially when, like our host, it begins with earnest, ceaseless work, and ends in reposing on millions; but it does not suit all. Above everything, it requires a clear, cool head, and yours does not appear to me to be quite made to devote itself to the grasping debit and credit. Excuse me, Herr Almbach! that is only my candid opinion; besides, I do not blame you at all for your daring. What would one not do to make a beautiful woman's obstinacy appear right! In this case, the manœ uvre was even *most agreeable*, any other person with the best will could not have carried it out; I congratulate you upon it."

He made a half-ironical bow, and left the room; it adjoined the drawing-room, but the half-closed *portières* divided it from the former; quite lonely and dimly-lighted, it offered a momentary solitude to whomsoever desired it. The young man had thrown himself upon a seat, and gazed dreamily before him. Of what he was thinking, perhaps he did not dare to confess to himself, and yet it was betrayed by his starting up at the sound of a voice, which said in a tone of slight astonishment--

"Ah, Signor Almbach, you here!"

It was Signora Biancona; whether, on entering, she had really not perceived who was already there, could not be decided, as she continued with perfect ease--

"I was seeking relief for a moment from the heat and whirl of the drawing-room. You, too, have soon withdrawn from the company after your triumph."

Almbach had risen, quickly. "If it is a question of triumph, there is certainly no doubt who gained it to-day. My improvised performance cannot be compared, in ever so slight a degree, with that which you offered to the public."

The Signora smiled. "I only produced sounds, like you, but I confess, candidly, it has surprised me, never, until to-night, and here, to meet an artist who surely long since--"

"Excuse me, Signora," interrupted the young man, coldly, "I have already declared in the drawing-room that I only lay claim to being a *dilettante*. I belong to the commercial world."

The same look of astonishment which he had seen on Welding's countenance in the theatre, was turned towards Almbach's face for the second time.

"Impossible! you are joking."

"Why impossible, Signora? Because I could play a difficult *bravura* piece with facility?"

"Because you could play it so, and because--" she looked at him fixedly for a moment, and then added, with great decision--"because your face bears the stamp one always imagines genius must carry on its brow."

"You see how deceptive appearances sometimes are."

Signora Biancona did not seem to agree with this; she sat down on the couch, her pale-coloured dress lay airily and lightly, as a cloud, on the dark velvet.

"I admire you," she began again, "that you are able, with such artistic qualities, to devote yourself to an every-day calling. It would be impossible for me; I have grown up in a world of sounds and tones, and cannot understand how there is room in it for any other duties."

This time there lay an undisguised bitterness in the young man's voice as he answered----"Also, your home is Italy; mine, a North-German business town! In our every-day life, poetry is a rare, fleeting guest, to whom a place is often refused. Work, striving after gain, stands ever in the foreground."

"With you, also, Signor?"

"It should, at least, stand there; that it is not always the case, my musical attempt will have shown you."

The singer shook her head doubtfully. "Your attempt! I should like to become acquainted with your finished work. But surely it cannot be your intention to withdraw this talent entirely from the public, and only exercise it in your home circle?"

"In my home circle!" repeated Almbach, with singular emphasis, "I do not touch a note there--least of all in my wife's presence."

"You are married already?" asked the Italian quickly, as a momentary pallor spread over her face.

"Yes, Signora."

This "yes," sounded dull and cold, and the half-mocking expression which played for a moment on the singer's lips, as she looked at the man of barely four-and-twenty years, disappeared at this tone.

"People marry very young in Germany, it appears," she remarked, quietly.

"Sometimes."

The young Italian seemed to find the pause which followed these words somewhat painful; she changed rapidly to another topic--

"I fear you have already been subjected to the examination of which I warned you. All the same, the company was charmed with your performance."

"Perhaps!" said the young man, half-contemptuously, "and yet it certainly was not intended for the company."

"Not! and for whom, then?" asked Signora Biancona, directing her glance firmly towards him. And he looked at her; there seemed to be something alike in both pairs of eyes which now met one another--both large, dark, and mysterious. In Almbach's glance, too, shone the same light as in the actress'; here also burned an ardent, passionate soul; also here, in the depths, slumbered the demonlike spark which is so often the heritage of genial natures, and becomes their curse when no protecting hand restrains it, and when it is fanned into flame, then no more brings light, but only destruction.

He came a step nearer and lowered his voice; its great excitement, however, still betrayed itself.

"Only for her, who, for me and for us all, a few hours since, embodied the highest beauty and the highest poetry, borne by the notes of an undying master-work. You have been worshipped a thousand-fold to-day, Signora. All that enthusiasm could offer was laid at your feet. The stranger, the unknown, also wished to tell you how much he admired you, and he did it in the language which alone is worthy of you. It is not quite strange to me either."

In his admiration there lay something that raised it above all flattery, the tone of real true enthusiasm, and Signora Biancona was actress enough to recognise this tone, woman enough to suspect what was hidden beneath it; she smiled with enchanting grace.

"I have seen, indeed, how very fluent you are in this language. Shall I not often hear it from you?"

"Hardly," said the young man, gloomily. "You return, as I hear, to Italy shortly, I--remain here in the North. Who knows if we shall ever meet again."

"Our manager intends to remain here until May," interrupted the Signora, quickly. "So our meeting to-day will surely not be our last? Certainly not--I count positively on seeing you again."

"Signora!" This passionate outbreak of Almbach's lasted only for a second. Suddenly a recollection or warning seemed to shoot through him; he drew back and bowed low and distantly.

"I fear it must be the last--farewell, Signora."

He was gone before it was possible for the singer to utter one word regarding this strange adieu, and he seemed to be in earnest about it, as not once during the whole evening did he approach the dangerous "circle of the sun."

CHAPTER II

"That is too bad. This mania really begins to surpass all limits. I must forbid Reinhold all cultivation of music if he continues to pursue it in so senseless a manner."

With these words, the merchant Almbach opened a family council, which took place in the parlour, in his wife's and daughter's presence, and at which, fortunately, the special object of the same did not assist.

Herr Almbach, a man about fifty, whose quiet, measured, almost pedantic manner, generally served as a pattern for all the office people, appeared to have quite lost his equilibrium to-day, by the above-named mania, as he continued, in great excitement--

"The bookkeeper came home this morning about four o'clock from the jubilee, which I had left directly after midnight. From the bridge he sees the garden house lighted up, and hears Reinhold raving over the notes, and lost to all sense of sight and hearing. Of course he could not accompany me to the feast! he declared himself to be ill; but his 'unbearable headache' did not hinder him from maltreating the piano in the icy-cold garden-room until morning's dawn. I shall be hearing again from my partners that my son-in-law has been doing his utmost in uselessness as well as in carelessness. It is hardly credible! The youngest clerk understands the books better, and has more interest in the business, than the partner and future head of the house of 'Almbach & Co.' My whole life long have I worked and toiled to make my firm secure and respected, and now I have the prospect of leaving it, at last, in such hands."

"I always told you that you should have forbidden his associating with the Music-Director, Wilkins," interrupted Frau Almbach, "he is to blame for it all; no one could get on with that misanthropical, musical fool. Everyone hated and avoided him, but with Reinhold that was all the more reason to form the most intimate friendship with him. Day after day he was there, and there alone was laid the foundation of all this musical nonsense, which his master seems to have bequeathed to him at his death. It is hardly bearable since he had the old man's legacy--the piano--in the house. Ella, what do you say, then, to this behaviour of your husband?"

The young wife, to whom the last words were addressed, had so far not spoken a syllable. She sat in the window, her head bent over her sewing, and only looked up as this direct question was addressed to her.

"I, dear mother?"

"Yes, you, my child, as the affair affects you most. Or do you really not feel the irresponsible manner in which Reinhold neglects you and your child?"

"He is so fond of music," said Ella, softly.

"Do you excuse him also?" said her mother, excitedly. "That is just the misfortune, he cares for it more than for wife or child; he never asks for either of you if he can only sit at his piano and improvise. Have you no idea of what a wife can and must demand from her husband, and that, above all, it is her duty to bring him to reason? But to be sure, nothing is ever to be expected of you."

The young wife certainly did not look as if much were to be expected of her. She had little that was attractive in her appearance, and the one thing about her that could perhaps be called pretty, the delicate, still girlishly slender figure, was entirely hidden under a most unbecoming house dress, which in its boundless plainness was more suggestive of a servant than of the daughter of the house, and was made so as to disguise any possible advantages which there might be. Only a narrow strip of the fair hair, which lay smoothly parted on her brow, was visible, the rest disappeared entirely under a cap more suited to her mother's years, and offering a peculiar contrast to the face of the barely twenty-years-old wife. This pale face with its downcast eyes, was not adapted to arouse any interest; it had no expression, there lay in it something stolid, vacant, that nearly approached to stupidity, and at this moment, when she let her sewing drop and looked at her mother, it betrayed such helpless nervousness and senselessness, that Almbach felt obliged to come to his daughter's assistance.

"Leave Ella alone!" said he in that half-angry, half-compassionate tone with which one rejects the interference of a child, "you know nothing is to be done with her, and what could she effect here?"

He shrugged his shoulders and continued bitterly; "That is the reward for the sacrifice of adopting my brother's orphan children! Hugo throws all gratitude, all reason and education in my face, and runs away secretly; and Reinhold, who has grown up in my house, under my eyes, causes me the greatest anxiety, with his good-for-nothing hankering after all fancies. But with him, at all events, I have kept the reins in my hand, and I shall draw them so tightly now, that he shall lose all inclination to chafe against them any more."

"Yes, Hugo's ingratitude was really outrageous!" Frau Almbach joined in. "To fly from our house at night, in a fog, and go to sea, 'to try his luck alone in the world,' as he said in the impudent letter of farewell which he left behind him! Two years since there actually came a letter to Reinhold from the Captain; and the former hinted only lately, quite openly, about his probable return. I fear he knows something positive about it."

"Hugo shall not cross my threshold," declared the merchant, with a solemn motion of his hand. "I know nothing of this interchange of letters with Reinhold, and will know nothing. Let them correspond behind my back, but if the unadvised youth should have the audacity to appear before me, he will learn what the anger of an offended uncle and guardian is."

While the parents prepared to discuss this apparently often-treated theme, with the wonted details and ire, Ella had left the room unnoticed and now descended the staircase leading to the office, situated on the ground floor. The young wife knew that now, at midday, all the people would be absent, and this probably lent her courage to enter.

It was a large gloomy room; whose bare walls and barred windows caused it somewhat to resemble a prison. No trouble had been taken to impart any comfort or even a pleasant appearance to the office. And what for? What belonged to work was there; the rest was luxury, and luxury was a thing that the house of Almbach and Co., notwithstanding its notoriously not inconsiderable wealth, did not allow itself.

At present no one was to be found in the room, excepting the young man, who sat at a desk with a big ledger open before him. He looked pale and as if he had been up late; his eyes, which should have been busy with figures, were fixed on the narrow strip of the sun's rays which fell slantingly across the room. In his gaze was something of the longing and bitterness of a prisoner, to whom the sunshine, penetrating into his cell, brings news of life and freedom from without. He hardly turned his head at the opening of the door, and asked indifferently--

"What is it? What do you want, Ella?"

Every other wife at the second question would have gone to her husband and put her arm round his shoulder. Ella remained standing close to the doorway. It sounded far too icily cold, this "What do you want?" she evidently was not welcome.

"I wished to ask how your headache is?" she began, shyly.

"My headache?" Reinhold recollected himself suddenly. "Ah, yes, I think it has gone."

The young wife closed the door and came a step or two nearer.

"My parents are very furious again, that you were not at the feast yesterday, and were playing, instead, the whole night long," she told him hesitatingly.

Reinhold knitted his brows. "Who told them? you perhaps?"

"I?" her voice sounded half like a reproach. "The bookkeeper saw the garden house lighted up, and heard you playing as he returned this morning."

An expression of contemptuous scorn played around the young man's lips, "Ah! I certainly had not thought of that. I did not believe that those gentlemen, after their jubilee, would have time or inclination left for observations. To be sure for spying they are always ready enough."

"My father thinks--" began Ella, again.

"What does he think?" shouted Reinhold. "Is it not enough for him that from morning to evening I am bound to this office; does he even grudge me the refreshment I seek at night in music? I thought that I and my piano had been banished far enough; that the garden house lay so distant and so isolated, that I could run no risk of disturbing the sleep of the righteous in the house. Fortunately no one can hear a sound."

"Not so," said the young wife, softly, "I hear every note when all is still around, and I alone lie awake."

Reinhold turned round and looked at his wife. She stood with downcast eyes and thoroughly expressionless face before him. His glance swept slowly down her figure as though he were unconsciously drawing some comparison, and the bitterness in his features became more plainly displayed.

"I am sorry for it," he replied coldly, "but I cannot help your windows looking into the garden. Close your shutters in future, then it is to be hoped that my musical extravagances will not disturb your sleep any more."

He turned over the pages of his book, and appeared to lose himself again in his calculations. Ella waited about a minute longer, but as she saw that not the least notice was taken of her presence, she went away as noiselessly as she came.

She had hardly left before Reinhold flung the ledger from him with a passionate movement. His glance, which fell upon the contemptuously-treated object, and was cast around the office, showed the most bitter hatred; then he laid his head on both arms and closed his eyes, as if he wished to see and hear no more of the whole surroundings.

"God greet you, Reinhold!" said a strange voice suddenly, quite close to him.

He started up, and looked bewildered and inquiringly at the stranger in sailor's clothes, who had entered unnoticed and now stood before him. Suddenly, however, a recollection seemed to shoot through him, as with a cry of joy, he threw himself on the new-comer's breast.

"Is it possible, Hugo!--you here already?"

Two powerful arms embraced him firmly, and a pair of warm lips were pressed again and again upon his.

"Do you really know me still? I should have picked you out from amongst hundreds. Certainly you do look rather different from the little Reinhold I left behind here. Well, with me I suppose it is not much better."

The first words still sounded full of deep emotion; but the latter already bore a somewhat merrier tone. Reinhold's arm still lay fondly round his brother's neck.

"And you come so suddenly, so completely unannounced? I only expected you in a few weeks' time."

"We have had an unusually quick voyage," said the young captain, cheerfully, "and once I was in the harbour, I could not stay a minute longer on board, I must come to you. Thank God, I found you alone! I was afraid I should have to pass the purgatorial fire of domestic anger and to fight my way through the united relatives in order to reach you."

Reinhold's face, still beaming with the pleasure of meeting again, became overcast at this recollection, and his arm fell slowly down.

"No one has seen you surely?" he asked, "you know how my uncle feels towards you, since--"

"Since I withdrew myself from his *all-wise* rule, which wished to screw me absolutely to the office table, and ran away?" interrupted Hugo. "Yes, I know; and I should have liked to look on at the row that broke loose in the house when they discovered I had fled. But the story is nearly ten years old. The 'good-for-nothing' is not dead and ruined, as the family have, no doubt, prophecied hundreds of times, and wished oftener; he returns as a most respected captain of a most splendid ship, with all possible recommendations to your principal houses of business. Should these mercantile and maritime advantages not at last soften the heart of the angry house of Almbach and Co.?"

Reinhold suppressed a sigh, "Do not joke, Hugo! you do not know my uncle--do not know the life in his house."

"No, I went away at the night time," asserted the Captain, "and that was most sensible; you should do the same."

"What are you thinking about? My wife--my child?"

"Ah yes!" said Hugo, somewhat confused. "I always forget you are married. Poor boy! they chained you fast by times. Such a betrothal altar is the safest bolt to thrust before all possible longing for freedom. There, do not fly out at once! I am quite willing to believe they did not regularly force you to say 'yes.' But how you came to do it, my uncle will probably have to answer for; and the melancholy attitude in which I found you, does not say much for the happiness of a young husband. Let me look into your eyes, that I may see how it really is."

He seized him unceremoniously by his arm, and drew him towards the window. Here in broad daylight, one could see, for the first time, how very unlike the brothers were, notwithstanding an undeniable resemblance in their features. The Captain, the elder of the two, was strongly, and yet gracefully built, his handsome, open countenance was browned by sun and air; his hair curled lightly, and his brown eyes sparkled with love of life and courage; his carriage was easy and firm, like that of a man accustomed to move in the most varied surroundings and circumstances, and his whole bearing had a species of self-confidence which broke forth at every opportunity, with, at the same time, such a fresh, open kindliness, that it was difficult to resist him.

Reinhold, his junior by a few years, made a totally different impression. He was slighter, paler than his brother; his hair and eyes were darker, and the latter had a serious, even gloomy expression. But there lay on this brow, and in those eyes, something which attracted all the more, as they did not disclose all which lay behind them. Hugo was, perhaps, the handsomer of the two, and yet a comparison was sure to be drawn unconditionally in favour of the younger brother, who possessed, in the highest degree, that rare and dangerous charm of being interesting, to which, often the most perfect beauty must give way.

The young man made a hasty attempt to withdraw from the threatened inspection. "You cannot remain here," he said, decidedly, "uncle may enter at any moment, and then there would be a terrible scene. I will take you to the garden house for the present, which I have had fitted up for my sole use.

You will hardly dare to appear before the family, and your arrival must be known. I will tell them."

"And bear all the storm alone?" interrupted the Captain. "I beg your pardon, but that is my affair! I am going up at once to my uncle and aunt, and shall introduce myself as their obedient nephew!"

"But Hugo! are you out of your senses? You have no idea of the state of affairs here."

"Exactly! The strongest fortresses are taken by surprise, and I have long looked forward to one day entering like a bomb amongst the stormy relations, and to seeing what sort of a grimace they would make. But one thing more. Reinhold, you must give me your promise to remain quietly below until I return. You shall not be placed in the painful position of witnessing how the weight of the family wrath is poured upon my erring head. You might wish to catch some of it out of brotherly self-sacrifice, and that would disturb all my plans of campaign. Jonas, come in!"

He opened the door and admitted a man, who, until now, had waited outside in the passage. "That is my brother. Look well at him! You have to report yourself to him, and pay him your respects. Once more, Reinhold, promise me not to enter the family parlour for the next half-hour. I shall bring all to order up there by myself, if I have even to take the whole barrack by storm."

He was out of the door before his brother could make any remonstrance. Still half-bewildered by the rapid changes of the last ten minutes, he looked at the broad, square figure of the new arrival, who set a good-sized portmanteau down on the floor, and planted himself close beside it.

"Seaman Wilhelm Jonas, of the 'Ellida,' now in the service of Herr Captain Almbach!" reported he, systematically, and attempted a movement at the same time, probably intended to be a bow, but which did not bear the least similarity to the desired courtesy.

"All right," said Reinhold, abruptly, "you can leave the luggage here at present! I must first hear how long my brother proposes remaining."

"We are to stay here a few days with his uncle," assured Jonas, very quietly.

"Oh! is that decided already?"

"Quite positively."

"I do not understand Hugo," murmured Reinhold. "He appears to have no idea of what is before him, and yet my letters must have prepared him for it. I cannot possibly let him bear the storm alone."

He made a movement towards the door, but this was quite blocked up by the sailor's broad figure, who, even at the young man's displeased glance of enquiry, did not move from his position.

"The Captain said that he would bring all to order up yonder by himself," he explained laconically, "so he will do it. He succeeds in everything."

"Really?" asked Reinhold, somewhat struck by the insuperable confidence of the words, "You seem to know my brother well."

"Very well."

Hesitating whether he should accede to Hugo's wish, Reinhold went to the window which looked into the court, and became aware of three or four faces, expressive of boundless curiosity, belonging to the servants, who were trying to obtain a peep into the office. The young man allowed a sound of suppressed annoyance to escape him, and turned again to the sailor.

"My brother's arrival seems to be known in the house already, said he hastily. Strangers are not such a rarity in the office, and the curiosity is evidently directed to you."

"It does not matter," muttered Jonas, "even if the whole nest becomes rebellious and stares at us. That sort of thing is nothing new. The savages in the South Sea Islands do just the same when our 'Ellida' lies-to."

The question may remain undecided, as to whether the comparison just drawn was exactly flattering to the inhabitants of the house. Fortunately no one but Reinhold heard it, and he considered it necessary to remove the object of this curiosity. He desired him to enter the adjoining room and wait there; he himself remained behind and listened uneasily if quarrelling voices were to be heard, but to be sure the family parlour lay in the upper story and at the other side of the house. The young man debated with himself as to whether he should remain true to the half-promise which he had made to Hugo, and leave him to manage alone, or if he should not, at least, attempt to cover the unavoidable retreat, as, that such lay before Hugo, he believed to be certain. He had too often heard the condemning verdict accorded to his brother by the family, not to dread a scene, in which even the former would be unable to hold his own, but he also knew his own position towards his uncle too well, not to say to himself that his interference would merely make matters worse.

More than half-an-hour had passed in this painful anxiety, when at last steps were heard and the Captain entered.

"Here I am, the affair is settled."

"What is settled?" asked Reinhold, hastily.

"Well, the pardon of course. As much-beloved nephew, I have this moment lain alternately in the arms of my uncle and aunt. Come upstairs with me, Reinhold! you are missing in the reconciliation *tableau*, but you must be prepared for endless emotion; they are all crying together."

His brother looked at him doubtfully. "I do not know, Hugo, if this be meant for fun, or--"

The young Captain laughed mischievously. "You seem to have little confidence in my diplomatic talents. But all the same, do not think that the affair was easily settled. I was certainly prepared for a storm. But here raged a regular tornado--bah, we sailors are accustomed to such things--and when at last I could obtain speech, which certainly was not for some time, the victory was already decided. I represented the return of the lost son with a masterly hand; I called heaven and earth as witnesses of my reformation. I ventured upon falling at their feet--that took, at least with my aunt--I now made sure of the hesitating female flank, in order to storm the centre in conjunction with it, and the victory was brilliant. Forgiveness in due form--general emotion and embraces--group of reconciliation--my Heaven, do not look so incredulous. I assure you I am speaking in all seriousness."

Reinhold shook his head, yet unconsciously he drew a breath of relief. "Comprehend it, who can! I should have thought it impossible! Have you"--the question sounded peculiarly uncertain--"have you seen my wife?"

"To be sure," said Hugo, slyly. "That is to say, I have certainly not seen much of her, and heard even less, as she remained quite passive during the scene, and did not even cry like the rest. The same little cousin Eleonore still, who always sat so quietly and shyly in her corner, out of which even our wildest boyish teasings did not drive her--and she has become your wife! But now, above all, I must admire the representative of the house of Almbach! Where is he?"

Reinhold looked up, and for a moment a bright gleam drove all the gloominess away from his face. "My boy? I will show him to you. Come, we will go up to him."

"Thank God, at last a sign of happiness in your face," said the Captain, with a seriousness of which one would hardly have deemed his merry nature capable, and he added in a lowered voice, "I have sought for it in vain so far."

The firm of Almbach and Co. belonged to that class whose names on the Exchange, as well as in the commercial world generally, were of some position, without being of conspicuous importance. The relations between its head and Consul Erlau were not only of a business nature; they dated from earlier times, when both, equally young and meanless, were apprenticed in the same office, the one to raise himself until he became a rich merchant, whose ships sailed on every ocean and whose connections extended to every quarter of the globe--the other to found a modest business, which never reached beyond certain bounds. Almbach avoided all more daring speculations, all greater undertakings, which he was by no means the man to superintend or guide; he preferred a moderate, but steady gain, which also fell to his share to the fullest extent. His social position was certainly as different from that of Consul Erlau as was his old-fashioned gloomy house in Canal Street, with its high gables and barred office windows, from the princely furnished palace at the Harbour. The friendship between the former youthful companions had gradually diminished, but it was certainly Almbach who was principally to blame for it. He could not be reconciled to the Consul after the latter had become a millionaire, living in the style suited to that position. Perhaps he could not forgive him for occupying the first place, while he himself only stood in the third or fourth rank, and well as he knew how to utilise the advantages which the intimate acquaintance with the great firm of Erlau opened to him, yet he held, all the more, to his strictly middle-class, and somewhat old-frankish household, and kept aloof from all communication with that of the Consul. The latter's invitations had ceased when he saw that they were never accepted; for years the mutual meetings had been restricted to those occasional ones on Exchange or some chance place, and lately Almbach had even, when any business matters required a personal interview, let his son-in-law represent him. It was decidedly disagreeable to him, that on this occasion the young man had received the invitation to the opera and the succeeding evening party, and impossible as it was to refuse this civility, the merchant did not attempt to disguise from his family his dissatisfaction at Reinhold's introduction into the "nabob's life," the designation with which he usually honoured his old friend's household.

Notwithstanding all this, Almbach was a well-to-do, even, as was maintained by many, a very rich man, and on this account the centre and support of numerous relations not blessed with over-much fortune. In this manner the care of his two orphaned nephews, whom their father, a ship's captain, had left quite without resources, fell to his charge. Almbach had only one child, to whose existence he had never attached very much importance, as she was a girl. The Consul and his wife were the little one's god-parents, and it might always be considered as an act of self-conquest, that Almbach gave his daughter Frau Erlau's name, as he particularly hated the aristocratic, romantic-sounding "Eleonore" and soon changed it for the much simpler "Ella." This designation was also more suitable, as Ella

Almbach was considered by every one to be, not only a simple, but even a very contracted-minded being, whose horizon never was extended beyond the trifling domestic events of housekeeping. The child had formerly been very sickly, and this may have had a crippling effect upon the development of her mental faculties. They were indeed of a very inferior order, and the very prejudiced, strictly domestic education in her father's house, excluding every other circle of ideas and thought, did not appear adapted to give them a higher direction. Thus, then, the girl had grown up quiet and shy, always overlooked, everywhere set aside, and without the least value, even amongst her nearest relations. They were wont to consider her quite incapable of self-dependence, even half-irresponsible, and her eventual marriage did not change things at all.

Neither of the young people raised any objection to the long-cherished, and to them long-known, plan of a union. A girl of seventeen and a man of twenty-two have certainly not much self-decision, least of all when they have grown up under such repressed circumstances. Besides, in this case, there was also the habit of always living together, which had created a sort of liking, although in Reinhold it was really only pitying tolerance, and in Ella secret fear of her mentally superior cousin. They gave their hands obediently at the betrothal, which was followed, after a year's reprieve, by the wedding. Almbach's sceptre swayed over both as much after as before it, he allowed his new son-in-law, who, as far as the name went, was literally his partner, as little independence in the business as his wife did the young mistress in the household.

CHAPTER III

It was Sunday morning. The office was closed, and Reinhold at last had a free morning before him, which certainly was seldom his good fortune. He was in the garden house, to the entire and special possession of which he had at last attained, to be sure only after many struggles and by repeated reference to his musical studies, which were considered highly disturbing in the house. It was here alone that the young man was in any degree safe from the constant control of his parents-in-law, which extended even into the young couple's dwelling, and he seized every free moment to take refuge in his asylum.

The so-called "garden" was of the only description possible in an old, narrowly-built, densely populated town. On all sides high walls and gables enclosed the small piece of ground, to which air and sunshine were sparingly given, and where a few trees and shrubs enjoyed but a miserable existence. The garden's boundary was one of those small canals, which traversed the town in all directions, and whose quick, dark stream formed a very melancholy background; beyond this, again, walls and gables were to be seen; the same prison-like appearance, which clung to Almbach's whole house seemed to reign over the only free space belonging to it.

The garden house itself was not much more cheerful--the single large room was furnished with more than simplicity. Evidently the few old-fashioned pieces of furniture had been set aside from some other place as superfluous, and been sought out in order to fit up the room with what was absolutely necessary. Only in the window, round which climbed some stunted vines, stood a large, handsome piano, the legacy of the late Music Director, Wilkens, to his pupil, and its magnificent appearance contrasted as singularly and strangely with the room as did the figure of the young man, with his ideal brow and large flashing eyes, behind the barred office windows of the dwelling-house.

Reinhold was sitting writing at the table, but to-day his face did not wear the tired, listless expression, which rested upon it whenever he had the figures of the account books before him; his cheeks were darkly, almost feverishly red, and as he wrote a name rapidly on the envelope, lying on the table, his hands trembled as if with suppressed excitement. Steps were heard outside, and the glass door was opened; with a quick gesture of annoyance the young man pushed the envelope under the sheets of music lying on the table, and turned round.

It was Jonas, servant of the Captain, who for a few days only had accepted the hospitality offered by his relations, and then had migrated to a dwelling of his own. The sailor saluted and entered in his peculiarly rough and somewhat uncouth manner, and then laid some books on the table.

"The Herr Captain's compliments, and he sends the promised books from his travelling library."

"Is my brother not coming himself?" asked Reinhold astonished. "He promised surely."

"The Captain has been here some time," replied Jonas, "but they have got hold of him in the house; your uncle wished to have a conference with him on family affairs; your aunt requires his help to make some alteration in the guest room, and the bookkeeper wants to catch him for his society. All are fighting for him; he cannot tear himself away."

"Hugo appears to have conquered the whole house in the course of a single week," remarked Reinhold ironically.

"We do that everywhere," said Jonas, full of self-consciousness, and appeared inclined to add more about those conquests, when he was interrupted by his master's entrance, who greeted his brother in the most cheerful humour.

"Good morning, Reinhold! Now Jonas, what are you staying here for? You are wanted in the house. I promised my aunt that you should help at the dinner to-day. Go at once to the kitchen!"

"Amongst the women!"

"Heaven knows," said Hugo, turning laughingly to his brother, "where this man has learned his hatred for women. Certainly not from me; I admire the lovely sex uncommonly."

"Yes, unfortunately, quite uncommonly," muttered Jonas, but he turned away obediently and marched out of the room, while the Captain came quite close to Reinhold.

"To-day there is a large family dinner!" he began, imitating his Uncle Almbach's pedantic, solemn voice so well as almost to deceive any one. "In my honour of course! I hope you will pay proper respect to this important ceremony, and that you will not again behave in such a manner, that I can at the utmost use you as a butt for my too developed amiability."

Reinhold knitted his brows slightly--

"I beg you, Hugo, do be sensible for once! How long do you intend to continue this comedy, and amuse yourself at the expense of the whole house? Take care, lest they find out what your amiability consists of, and that you are really only ridiculing them all."

"That would indeed be bad," said Hugo, quietly, "but they will not find me out, depend upon that."

"Then do me the kindness, at least, of ceasing your horrid Indian tales! You really go too far with them. Uncle was debating with the bookkeeper yesterday about the battle with the monster serpent, which you served up for them lately, and which, even to him, appeared unheard of. I became extremely confused in listening to them."

"It put you to confusion?" mocked the Captain. "If I had been there, I should immediately have given them the benefit of an elephant hunt, a tiger story, and a few attacks of savages, with such appalling effects, that the affair of the giant snake would have appeared highly probable to them. Be easy! I know my hearers; the whole house oppresses me almost, with its acts of sympathy."

"Excepting Ella," suggested Reinhold, "it is certainly remarkable that her shyness towards you is quite invincible."

"Yes, it is very remarkable," said Hugo with an offended air. "I cannot allow any one in the house to exist who is not entirely persuaded of my perfections, and have already set myself the task of presenting myself to my sister-in-law in all my utterly irresistible charms. I do not doubt at all that she will thereupon immediately join the majority--you are not jealous, I hope."

"Jealous?--I? and on Ella's account?" The young man shrugged his shoulders half-pityingly, half-contemptuously.

"What are you thinking of?"

"Well, there is no danger! I have sought an interview with her already, but she was entirely occupied with the young one. Tell me, Reinhold, where does the child get those wonderful, blue, fairy-tale-like eyes from? Yours are not so, besides there is not the least resemblance, and, excepting his, I do not know any in the family."

"I believe Ella's eyes are blue," interrupted his brother indifferently.

"You believe only? Have you never convinced yourself then? Certainly it may be somewhat difficult; she never raises them, and, under that monstrous cap, nothing can be seen of her face. Reinhold, for Heaven's sake, how can you allow your wife such an antediluvian costume? I assure you, for me that cap would be grounds sufficient for a divorce."

Reinhold had seated himself at the piano, and let his hands glide mechanically over the notes, while he answered with perfect indifference--

"I never trouble myself about Ella's toilet, and I believe it would be useless to try and enforce any alterations there. What does it matter to me?"

"What it matters to you how your wife looks?" repeated the Captain, as he seized some sheets of music on the table, and turned them over lightly, "a charming question from a young husband! You used to have a sense of beauty, too easily aroused, and I could almost fear--what is this then? 'Signora Beatrice Biancona on it.' Have you Italian correspondents in the town?"

Reinhold sprang up, confusion and annoyance struggled in his face, as he saw the letter, which he had pushed under the music, in his brother's hands, who repeated the address unconcernedly.

"Beatrice Biancona? That is the *prima donna* of the Italian Opera, who has made such a wonderful sensation here? Do you know the lady?"

"Slightly," said Reinhold, taking the letter quickly from his hands. "I was introduced to her lately at Consul Erlau's."

"And you correspond with her already?"

"Certainly not! The letter does not contain one single line."

Hugo laughed aloud, "An envelope fully addressed, a very voluminous sheet of paper inside it, with not a single line! Dear Reinhold, that is more wonderful than my story of the giant snake. Do you expect me really to believe it? There, do not look so savage, I do not intend to force myself into your secrets."

Instead of answering, the young man drew the paper out of the unsealed envelope, and held it to his brother, who looked at it in astonishment.

"What does it mean? Only a song--notes and words--no word of explanation with it--just your name below. Have you composed it?"

Reinhold took the paper again, closed the letter and put it in his pocket.

"It is an attempt, nothing more. She is *artiste* enough to judge of it. She can accept or reject it."

"Then you compose also?" asked the Captain, whose face had become serious all at once. "I did not think that your passionate liking for music went so far as creating it yourself. Poor Reinhold, how can you bear this life, with all its narrow, confined ways, wishing to stifle every spark of poetry as being unnecessary or dangerous? I could not do it."

Reinhold had thrown himself upon the seat before the piano again.

"Do not ask me how I endure it," he replied, with suppressed feeling. "It is enough *that* I do it."

"I guessed long since that your letters were not open," continued Hugo; "that behind all the contentment with which you tried to deceive me, something quite different was concealed. The truth has become plain to me, during one week in this house, notwithstanding that you gave yourself all conceivable trouble to hide it from me."

The young man gazed gloomily before him. "Why should I worry you, when far away, with anxieties about me? You had enough to do to take care of yourself, and there was a time, too, when I was contented, or at least believed myself so, because my whole mental being lay, as it were, under a spell, when I allowed everything to pass over me in stupid indifference, and I offered my hand willingly for the chain. I have done it; well, yes! But I must carry it my whole life long!"

Hugo had gone towards him, and laid his hand upon his brother's shoulder.

"You mean your marriage with Ella? At the first news of it, I knew it must be my uncle's work."

A bitter smile played round the young man's lips as he answered scornfully--

"He was always a splendid master of calculation, and he has shown it again in this case. The poor relation, taken up out of kindness and charity, must consider it happiness that he is raised to be son and heir of the house, and the daughter must be married some time; so it was a case of securing, by means of her hand, a successor for the firm, who bore the same name. It was neither Ella's nor my fault that we were bound together. We were both young, without wills, without knowledge of life or of ourselves. She will always remain so--well for her. It has not been so fortunate for me."

One would hardly have credited those merry brown eyes with the power of looking so serious as at this moment, when he bent down to his brother.

"Reinhold," said he, in an undertone, "on the night when I fled to save myself from a caprice, which would have ruined my freedom and future, I had planned and foreseen everything, excepting one, the most difficult-

-the moment when I should stand by your bed to bid you farewell. You slept quietly, and did not dream of the separation; but I--when I saw your pale face on the pillow, and said to myself that for years, perhaps never again, should I see it, all longing for freedom could not resist it--I struggled hard with the temptation to awake and take you with me. Later, when I experienced the thorny path of the adventurous homeless boy, with all its dangers and privations, I often thanked God that I had withstood the temptation; I knew you were safe and sound in our relation's house, and now"--Hugo's strong voice trembled as with suppressed anger or pain--"now I wish I had carried you with me to want and privation, to storm and danger, but at any rate to freedom; it had been better."

"It had been better," repeated Reinhold, listlessly; then rising as if reckless, "Let us cease! What is the use of regrets, which cannot change what is past. Come! They expect us upstairs."

"I wish I had you on my 'Ellida,' and we could turn our backs on the whole crew, never to see them again," said the young sailor, with a sigh, as he prepared to follow his brother's bidding. "I never thought things could be so bad."

The brothers had hardly entered the house, when Hugo's indispensability began to show itself again. He was in request, at least on three sides, at once. Every one required his advice and help. The young Captain appeared to possess the enviable power of throwing himself directly from one mood into another, as, immediately after his serious conversation with his brother, he was sparkling with merriment and mischief, helped every one, paid compliments to each, and at the same time teased all in the most merciless manner. This time it was the bookkeeper who caught him, as Jonas expressed it, to explain the affairs of his society; and while the two gentlemen were discussing it, Reinhold entered the dining-room, where he found his wife busied with preparations for the before-named guests.

Ella was in her Sunday costume to-day, but that made little alteration in her appearance. Her dress of finer material was not more becoming; the cap, which inspired her brother-in-law with such horror, surrounded and disfigured her face as usual. The young wife devoted herself so assiduously and completely to her domestic duties, that she hardly seemed to notice her husband's entrance, who approached her with rather lowering mien.

"I must beg you, Ella," he began, "to have more regard for my wishes in future, and to meet my brother in such a manner as he can and would expect his sister-in-law to do. I should think that the behaviour of your parents, and every one in the house, might serve as an example for you; but you appear to find an especial pleasure in denying him every right of relationship, and in showing him a decided antipathy."

The young wife looked as timid and helpless at this anything but kindly expressed reproof, as she did when her mother desired her to interfere about her husband's musical "mania."

"Do not be angry, dear Reinhold," she replied, hesitatingly, "but I--I cannot do otherwise."

"You cannot?" asked Reinhold, sharply. "Of course, that is your never-failing answer when I ask anything of you, and I should have thought it was seldom enough that I do address a request to you. But this time I insist positively that you should change your demeanour towards Hugo. This shy avoidance and consequent silence whenever he speaks to you is too ridiculous. I beg seriously that you will take more care not to make me appear too much an object of pity to my brother."

Ella appeared about to answer, but the last unsparing words closed her lips. She bowed her head, and did not make any further attempt to defend herself. It was a movement of such gentle, patient resignation as would have disarmed any one; but Reinhold did not notice it, as at the same moment the old bookkeeper was heard taking leave in the next room.

"Then we may count upon the honour of your membership, Herr Captain? And as regards the election of a President, I have your word that you will support the opposition?"

"Quite at your service," said Hugo's voice, "and of course only with the opposition. I always join the opposition on principle whenever there is one; it is generally the only faction in which there is any fun. Excuse me, the honour is on my side."

The bookkeeper left, and the Captain appeared in the room. He seemed inclined to redeem the promise he had given to his brother, and at the same time to convince the young wife of his perfections, as he approached her with all the boldness and confidence of his nature, with which a certain knightly gallantry was mingled.

"Then I owe it to chance that at last I see my sister-in-law, and she is compelled to remain with me a few moments? Certainly she never would have accorded me this happiness of her own free will. I was complaining bitterly to Reinhold this morning about your repelling me, which I do not know that I have merited in any way."

He wished to take her hand, even to kiss it, but Ella drew back, with a, for her, quite unwonted decision.

"Herr Captain!"

"Herr Captain!" repeated Hugo, annoyed. "No, Ella, that is going too far. I certainly, as your brother, have a right to the 'thou' which you never refused to your cousin and childish companion, but as you, from the first day of my arrival, laid so much stress on the formal 'you,' I followed the hint you gave me. However, this 'Herr Captain' I will not stand. That is an insult against which I shall call Reinhold to my assistance. He shall tell me if I must really bear hearing myself being called 'Herr Captain' by those lips."

"Certainly not!" said Reinhold, as he turned to leave, "Ella will give up this manner of speaking to you, as well as her whole tone towards you. I have just been speaking distinctly to her about it."

He went away, and his glance ordered his wife to remain, as plainly as his voice demanded obedience. Neither escaped the Captain.

"For goodness sake, do not interfere with your husband's authority! Would you command friendliness towards me?" cried he after his brother, and turned again quickly to Ella, while he continued, gallantly, "that would be the surest way to prevent my ever finding favour in my beautiful sister-in-law's eyes. But that is not required between us, is it? You will permit me, at least, to lay the due tribute of respect at your feet, to describe to you the joyful surprise with which I received the news--"

Here Hugo stopped suddenly, and seemed to have lost his train of ideas. Ella had raised her eyes, and looked at him. It was a gleam of quiet, painful reproach, and the same reproach lay in her voice as she replied, "At least leave me in peace, Herr Captain. I thought you had amusement enough for to-day."

"I?" asked Hugo, taken aback. "What do you mean, Ella? You do not think--"

The young wife did not let him finish. "What have we done to you?" she continued, and although her voice trembled timidly at first, it gained firmness with every word. "What have we done to you that you always scoff at us, since the day of your return, when you acted a scene of repentance before my parents, until the present moment, when you make the whole house the target for your jokes? Reinhold certainly tolerates our being daily humiliated; he looks upon it as a matter of course. But I, Herr Captain--" here Ella's voice had attained perfect steadiness, "I do not consider it right that you should daily cast scorn and contempt over a house in which you, after all that has passed, have been received with the old love. If this house and family do appear so very meagre and ridiculous to you, no one invited you here. You should have remained in that world of which you are able to relate so much. My parents deserve more respect and mercy even for their weaknesses; and, although our house may be simple, it is still too good for the scoffs of an--adventurer."

She turned her back upon him, and left the room without waiting for a single word of reply. Hugo stood and gazed after her, as if one of the impossible scenes out of his own Indian stories had just been acted before him. Probably, for the first time in his life, the young sailor lost, with his presence of mind, the power of speech also.

"That was plain," said he at last, as he sat down, quite upset; but the next moment he sprang up as if electrified, and cried--

"She has them in truth; the child's beautiful blue eyes. And I discovered them only now! Who, indeed, would look for this glance under that horrible cap? 'We are too good for the scoffs of an adventurer.' Not exactly flattering, but it was merited, although I expected least of all to hear it from her! I shall often try that."

Hugo moved as if going into the guest room, but he stopped again on the threshold, and looked towards the door, by which his sister-in-law had retired. All signs of mockery and mischief had entirely vanished from his face; it bore a thoughtful expression as he said, gently, "And Reinhold only *believes* she has blue eyes! Incomprehensible!"

In the large concert-room of H----, all the *elite* of the town seemed to be gathered on the occasion of one of those concerts which, set on foot for some charitable purpose, were patronised by the first families, and whose support and presence there was considered quite a point of honour. To-day the programme only bore well-known names, both as regarded the performances as well as performers; and besides, it was arranged by means of the highest possible prices that the audience should consist principally, if not entirely, of persons belonging to the best circles of society.

The concert had not commenced, and the performers were in a room adjoining, which served as a place of assembly on such occasions, and to which only a few specially favoured of the outside world had the right of entrance. Therefore the presence was the more remarkable of a young man who did not belong either to the favoured or the performers, and who kept aloof from both. He had entered shortly before and addressed himself at once to the conductor, who, although he did not appear to know him, yet must have been informed of his coming, as he received him very politely. The gentlemen around only heard so much of the conversation, that the conductor regretted not to be able to give Mr. Almbach any information: it was Signora Biancona's wish; the Signora would appear directly. The short interview was soon over, and Reinhold drew back.

The group of artists, engaged in lively conversation, broke up suddenly, as the door opened and the young *prima donna* appeared; she had not been expected so soon, as she usually only drove up at the last moment. Every one began to move. All tried to outdo one another in attentions to their beautiful colleague, but to-day she took remarkably little notice of the wonted homage of her surroundings. Her glance on entering had flown rapidly through the room, and had at once found the object of its search. The Signora deigned to reply to the greetings only very slightly, exchanged a few words with the conductor, and withdrew at once from all further attempts at conversation with the gentlemen, as she turned to Reinhold Almbach, who now approached her, and went towards the farthest window with him.

"You have really come, Signor?" she began in a reproachful tone, "I did not believe, indeed, that you would accept my invitation."

Reinhold looked up, and the forced coldness and formality of the greeting began already to melt as he met her gaze for the first time on that evening.

"Then it was your invitation," he said. "I did not know if I was to consider the one sent by the conductor in your name, as such. It did not contain a single line from you."

Beatrice smiled. "I only followed the example set me. I, too, have received a certain song, whose composer added nothing to his name. I only retaliated."

"Has my silence offended you?" asked the young man, quickly. "I dared add nothing. What--" his eyes sank to the ground--"what should I have said to you?"

The first question was indeed unnecessary; as the devotion of the song seemed to have been understood, and Signora Biancona looked the reverse of offended as she answered--

"You appear to like the wordless form, Signor, and always to wish to speak to me in notes of music. Well, I bowed to your taste, and have determined to answer also only in our language."

She laid a slight but still marked emphasis upon the word. Reinhold raised his head in astonishment.

"In our language?" he repeated slowly.

CHAPTER IV

Beatrice drew a paper out of the roll of music which she held in her hand. "I have waited in vain for the author of this song to come to me, in order to hear it from my lips and receive my thanks for it. He has left to strangers that which was his duty. I am accustomed to *be sought*, Signor. You seem to expect the same."

There certainly lay some reproach in her voice, but it was not very harsh, and it would have been hardly possible, as Reinhold's eye betrayed only too plainly what this staying away had cost him. He made no reply to the reproach, did not defend himself against it, but his glance, which seemed magnetically bound by the brilliantly beautiful apparition, told her that his self-restraint was caused by anything rather than indifference.

"Do you think I have sent for you to hear the air which is put down in the programme?" continued the Italian, playfully. "The audience always desires this air *da capo*; it is too trying for a repetition; I propose, therefore, instead of this, to sing--something else."

A deep glow covered the young man's features, and he stretched out his hand, as if with an unconscious movement, towards the paper.

"For mercy's sake! surely not my song?"

"You are uncommonly alarmed about it," said the singer, stepping back, and withdrawing the music from him. "Are you afraid for the fate of your work in my hands?"

"No, no!" cried Reinhold passionately, "but--"

"But? No objections, Signor! The song is dedicated to me, is handed over to me for good or evil. I shall do with it what I choose. Only one more question. The director is quite prepared; we have practised the performance together, but I should prefer seeing you at the piano when I appear before the audience with your music. May I count upon you?"

"You will trust yourself to my accompaniment?" asked Reinhold, with trembling voice. "Trust yourself entirely without first trying it? That is a risk for us both."

"Only if your courage fail, not otherwise," explained Beatrice. "With your power over the piano I have already made acquaintance, and there is certainly no question as to whether you are sure of the accompaniment to your work. If you are as sure of yourself before this audience as you were lately at the party, we can perform the song without hesitation."

"I will risk all, if you are at my side," Reinhold exclaimed, passionately. "The song was written for you, Signora. If you decide differently for it, its fate lies in your hand. I am ready for all."

She answered only with a smile, proud and confident of success, and turned to the conductor who at that moment drew near. Then ensued a low, but lively conversation in the group, and the other gentlemen regarded with undisguised displeasure the young stranger who quite monopolised the attention and conversation of the Signora and, to their great annoyance, occupied her until the signal for the commencement of the concert was given.

The room, in the meanwhile, had filled to the very last seat, and the dazzlingly-lighted place, in conjunction with the rich toilets of the ladies, offered a brilliant sight. Consul Erlau's wife sat with several other ladies in the front part of the room, and was engaged in conversation with Dr. Welding, when her husband, accompanied by a young man, wearing a captain's uniform, came up to her seat.

"Herr Captain Almbach," he said, introducing him, "to whom I owe the rescue of my best ship and all its crew. It was he who came to the help of the 'Hansa,' when already almost foundered, and it is entirely to his self-sacrificing energy--"

"Oh pray, Herr Consul, do not let Frau Erlau immediately anticipate a storm at sea!" interrupted Hugo, "we poor sailors are always so maligned as regards our adventures, that every lady looks forward with secret horror to their inevitable relation. I assure you though, Madame, that you have nothing to fear with me. I intend my conversational attempts to be confined to the mainland."

The young sailor appeared indeed to understand very thoroughly the differences of the society in which he moved. It never entered his head here, when the opportunity was offered him, to recount adventures, which in his relative's house he lavished so liberally. The Consul shook his head a little dissatisfied.

"You appear wishful to laugh away all recognition of your services," responded he. "I am not the less in your debt, even if you do make it impossible for me to discharge it in any way. Besides, I do not believe the relation of this adventure would injure you with the ladies, quite the contrary. And as you refuse all account of it so positively, I shall reserve it myself for the next opportunity."

Frau Erlau turned with winning friendliness to Hugo.

"You are no stranger to us, Herr Captain Almbach, even for your family's sake. Only lately we had the pleasure of seeing your brother at our house."

"Yes--only once," added the Consul, "and then merely by chance. Almbach appears unable to forgive me that my mode of living varies so from his own. He purposely keeps himself and all his family at a distance, and for years has stopped all visits from our godchild--we hardly know what Eleanor looks like."

"Poor Eleanor!" remarked Frau Erlau, compassionately. "I fear she has been intimidated by a too strict bringing up, and being kept much too secluded. I never see her otherwise than shy and quiet, and I believe in the presence of strangers she never raises her eyes."

"She does though," said Hugo, in a peculiar voice. "She does sometimes, but certainly I doubt if my brother has ever seen her do so."

"Your brother is not here, then?" asked the lady.

"No. He declined to accompany me. I do not understand it, as I know his infatuation for music and especially for Biancona's singing. I am to see this sun of the south, whose rays dazzle all H----, rise to-day for the first time."

The Consul cautioned him laughingly with his finger.

"Do not scoff, Captain; rather protect your own heart against these rays. To you, young gentleman, such things are most dangerous. You would not be the first who had succumbed to the magic of those eyes."

The young sailor laughed confidently.

"And who says then, Herr Consul, that I fear such a fate? I always succumb in such cases with the greatest pleasure, and the consolatory knowledge that the magic is only dangerous for him who flees it. Whoever stands firm, is generally soon disenchanted, often sooner than he wishes."

"It appears you have had great experience already in such affairs," said Frau Erlau, with a touch of reproof.

"My God, Madame, when year after year one flies from country to country, and never takes root anywhere, is nowhere so much at home as on the rolling, ever-moving sea, one learns to look upon constant change as inevitable, and at last to love it. I expose myself entirely to your displeasure with this confession, but I must really beg of you to look upon me as a savage, who has long forgotten, in tropical seas and countries, how to satisfy the requirements of North German civilisation."

Yet the manner in which the young Captain bowed and kissed the lady's hand as he spoke, betrayed a sufficient acquaintance with these requirements, and Dr. Welding remarked, drily, as he turned to the Consul--

"The tropical barbarism of this gentleman will not distinguish itself very badly in our drawing-rooms. So the hero of the much talked of 'Hansa' affair is really the brother of the young Almbach to whom Signora Biancona is just now according an interview in the assembly-room?"

"Whom? Reinhold Almbach?" asked Erlau, astonished. "You heard just now that he is not here."

"Certainly not, according to the Herr Captain's views," said Welding, quietly. "According to mine, he positively is. Pray do not mention it! To-night's concert seems intended to bring us some surprise. I have a certain suspicion, and we shall see if it be well-founded or not. The Signora likes theatrical effects, even off the stage; everything must be unexpected, lightning-like, overwhelming; a prosaic announcement would spoil everything. The conductor is, of course, in the plot, but was not so easily persuaded. We shall await it."

He ceased, as Hugo, who until now had been talking to the ladies, came to them, and immediately after the concert commenced.

The first part and half of the second passed, according to the programme, with more or less lively interest for the audience. Only towards the close did Signora Biancona appear, whose performance, notwithstanding all that had so far been heard, formed the point of attraction of the evening. The audience received and greeted their favourite, whose pale features were more charming than ever, with loud applause. Beatrice was indeed radiantly beautiful as she stood under the streaming light of the chandelier, in a flowing gauze dress strewn with flowers, and roses in her dark hair. She acknowledged it with smiling thanks on all sides, and, when the conductor, who undertook the accompaniment, had seated himself at the piano, began her recitative.

This time it was one of those grand Italian *bravura* airs, which at every concert and on every stage are certain of success, and demand the audience's applause without at the same time fulfilling higher requirements. A number of brilliant passages and effects made up for the depth, which was really wanting in the composition, but it offered the Italian an opportunity for perfect display of her magnificent voice. All these runs and trills fell clearly as a bell from her lips, and took such entrancing possession of the hearers' ears and senses, that all criticism, all more serious longings, vanished in the pure enjoyment of listening. It was a charming playing with tones--to be sure, only playing, nothing more--but combined with the finished certainty and grace of the performance, it acted like electricity upon the audience, who overwhelmed the singer more lavishly than usual with applause, and stormily encored the air *da capo*.

Signora Biancona seemed also inclined to accede to this wish as she came forward again, but at the same moment the conductor left the piano, and a young man, who had hitherto not been observed among the other performers, took his place. The spectators stared in astonishment, the Consul and his wife gazed at him in surprise; even Hugo at the first moment looked almost shocked at his brother, whose presence he had not suspected, but he began to guess at the connection. Only Dr. Welding said quietly, and without the least surprise, "I thought it!" Reinhold looked pale, and his hands trembled on the keys; but Beatrice stood at his side--a softly-whispered word from her mouth, a glance out of her eyes, gave him back his lost courage. He began the first chords steadily and quietly, which at once told the audience it was not to be a repetition of their favourite piece. All listened wonderingly and eagerly, and then Beatrice joined in.

That was certainly something very different from the *bravura* air just heard. The melodies which now flowed forth had nothing in common with those runs and trills, but they made their way to the hearers' hearts. In those tones, which now rose as in stormy rejoicing, and again sank in sad complaint, there seemed to breathe the whole happiness and sorrow of a human life; a long-fettered yearning seemed at last to struggle forth. It was a language of affecting power and beauty, and if it was not quite understood by all, yet all felt that there was a sound of something powerful, everlasting in it; even the most indifferent superficial crowd cannot remain void of feeling when genius speaks to it.

And here genius had found its mate, who knew how to follow and perfect it. There was no more talk of a risk for both, as the one met the idea of the other. The most careful study could not have given so perfect a mutual understanding as was here created in a moment and by inspiration. Reinhold found himself comprehended in every note, grasped at every turn, and never had Beatrice sung so enchantingly, never had the spirit of her singing displayed itself so much. She took her part with glowing *abandon*; the talent of the singer and the dramatic power of the actress flowed together. It was a performance which would have ennobled even the most insignificant composition--here it became a double triumph.

The song was ended. The breathless silence with which it had been listened to continued a few seconds longer; no hand moved, no sign of applause was heard; but then a storm broke forth, such as even the *fêted prima donna* had seldom heard, and at any rate is unknown in a concert-room. Beatrice seemed only to have waited for this moment; in the next she had stepped to Reinhold, seized his hand, and drawn him with her to the foot-lights, introducing him to the audience. This one movement said enough; it was understood at once that the composer stood before them. The storm of applause for both raged anew, and the young musician, still half-bewildered by the unexpected success, holding Beatrice's hand, received the first greeting and first approbation of the crowd.

Reinhold only returned clearly to consciousness in the assembly-room, whither he had accompanied Signora Biancona; a few moments of solitude still remained to him; beyond, in the concert-room, the orchestra was playing the finale to a most indifferent audience, which was still completely impressed by what it had just heard. Beatrice withdrew her arm which lay in that of her companion.

"We have conquered," she said, softly; "were you satisfied with my song?"

With a passionate movement, Reinhold seized both her hands, "Ask not this question, Signora! Let me thank you, not for the triumph, which was more yours than mine, but that I was also permitted to hear my song from your lips. I composed it in the recollection of you--for you alone, Beatrice. You have understood what it says to you, otherwise you could not have sung it in such a manner."

Signora Biancona may have understood it only too well, but in the glance with which she looked down at him there lay still more than the mere triumph of a beautiful woman, who has again proved the irresistibility of her power. "Do you say that to the woman, or the actress?" asked she, half-playfully. "The road is now open, Signor, will you follow it?"

"I will," declared Reinhold, raising himself determinedly, "whatever opposes me, and whatever form my future may take, it will have been consecrated for me, since the Goddess of Song herself opened the gate to me."

The last words had the same tone of passionate adulation which Beatrice heard from him once before; she bent closer towards him, and her voice sounded soft, almost beseeching, as she answered--

"Do not then avoid the Goddess any more so obstinately as hitherto. The composer will surely be allowed to come to the actress from time to time. If I study your next work, Signor, shall I have to discover its meaning alone again, or will you stand by me this time?"

Reinhold gave no reply, but the kiss which he pressed burningly hot upon her hand, did not say no. Nor did he this time bid her farewell--this time no recollection tore him away from the dangerous proximity. Whatever arose in the distance that time with gentle warning, had now no place in a single thought of the young man's mind. How could, indeed, the faint, colourless picture of his young wife exist near a Beatrice Biancona, who stood before him in all the witch-like charms of her being, this "Goddess of Song," whose hand had just conducted him to his first triumph! He saw and heard her only. What for years had lain hidden within him--what, since his meeting with her had struggled and fought its way out, this evening decided the beginning of an artist's career, and of a family drama.

The following days and weeks in the Almbachs' house were not the most agreeable. It could naturally not remain concealed from the merchant that his son-in-law had appeared before the public with his composition, and for this reason, that Dr. Welding, in the morning paper, gave a detailed account of the concert, in which the name of the young composer was mentioned. But neither the praise which the usually severe critic accorded in this instance, nor the approval with which the song was everywhere received, nor even the intervention of Consul Erlau, who, taking Reinhold's part very eagerly and decidedly, upheld his musical gifts, could overcome Almbach's prejudices. He persisted in seeing in all artistic efforts an idling as useless as it was dangerous--the real ground of all incapacity for practical business life, and the root of all evil. Knowing as little as most people that it had been almost an act of compulsion by which Signora Biancona had forced Reinhold to appear publicly, he regarded the whole as a pre-arranged affair, which had been undertaken without his knowledge and against his will, and which made him almost beside himself. He allowed himself to be so carried away, that he called his son-in-law to account like a boy, and forbade him, once for all, any farther musical pursuits.

That was, of course, the worst thing he could have done. At this prohibition, Reinhold broke out into uncontrollable defiance. The passion which, despite all that fettered it outwardly and held it in bounds, formed the groundwork of his character now broke out into a truly terrific fury. A fearful scene ensued, and had Hugo not interposed with quick thought, the breach would have become quite irremediable. Almbach saw with horror that the nephew whom he had brought up and led, whom he had tied to himself by every possible bond of family and business, had outgrown his control completely, and never thought of bending to his power. The strife had ceased for the time present, but only to break out afresh at the first opportunity. One scene succeeded another; one bitterness surpassed another.

Reinhold soon stood in opposition to his whole surroundings, and the defiance with which he clung more than ever to his musical studies, and maintained his independence out of the house, only increased the anger of his father and mother-in-law.

Frau Almbach, who shared her husband's opinion entirely, supported him with all her strength; Ella, on the contrary, remained, as usual, quite passive. Any interference or taking a part was neither expected nor desired; her parents never thought of crediting her with the very least influence over Reinhold, and he himself ignored her in this affair altogether, and did not even seem to grant her the right of offering an opinion. The young wife suffered undeniably under these circumstances; whether she felt the sad, humiliating part which she, the wife, played--thus overlooked by both factions--set aside and treated as if incapable--could hardly be decided. At her parents' bitter and excited discussions, and her husband's constant state of irritation, which often found vent at trifling causes, and was generally directed against her, she always showed the same calm, patient resignation, seldom uttered a beseeching word, never interfered by any decided partisanship, and when, as usual, roughly repulsed, drew back more shyly than ever.

The only one who remained now, as before, on the best terms with all, and kept his undisputed place as general favourite, was, strange to say, the young Captain. Like all obstinate people, Almbach resigned himself more easily to a fact than to a struggle, and forgave more easily the direct but quiet want of regard for his authority, such as his eldest nephew had shown him, than the stormy opposition to his will which was now attempted by the younger one. When Hugo saw that a hated calling was forced upon him, he had neither defied nor offended his uncle; he had simply gone away, and let the storm rage itself out behind his back. Certainly, he did not hesitate later to enact the return of the prodigal son to ensure his entrance into the house to which his brother belonged, and his restoration to his relations' favour. Reinhold possessed neither the capability nor the inclination to play with circumstances in this way. Just as he had never been able to disguise his dislike to business life, and his indifference to all the provincial town interests, so he now made no secret of his contempt for all around him, his burning hatred for the fetters which confined him--and it was this which could not be pardoned. Hugo, who espoused his brother's side positively, was permitted to take his part openly, and did so on every occasion. His uncle pardoned him this, even looked upon it as quite natural, as the young Captain's mode of treatment never let it come to a rupture, while with

Reinhold, the subject only needed to be touched upon in order to cause the most furious scenes between him and his wife's parents.

It was about noontide, when Hugo entered the Almbachs' house, and met his servant, whom he had sent before with a message to his brother, at the foot of the stairs. Jonas was really nominally only a sailor in the "Ellida;" he had long had his discharge from the ship, and been appointed solely to the young Captain's personal service, whom he never left, even during a lengthy stay on shore, and whom he followed everywhere with constant, unvarying attachment. Both were of about the same age. Jonas was truly far from ugly; in his Sunday clothes he might even pass for a good-looking fellow, but his uncouth manner, his rough ways and his chariness of speech never allowed these advantages to be perceived. He was almost on an enemy's footing with all the servants, especially the women of Almbach's household, and none of them had ever seen a pleasant expression on his face, nor heard a word more than was absolutely necessary. Even now he looked very sour, and the four or five dollars he was just counting in his hand seemed to excite his displeasure, judging from the savage way he looked at them.

"What is it, Jonas?" asked the Captain, approaching, "are you taking stock of your ready money?"

The sailor looked up, and put himself in an attitude of attention, but his face did not become more pleasant.

"I am to go to the nursery garden and get a bouquet of flowers," he grumbled, as he put the money in his pocket.

"Oh! are you employed as messenger for flowers?"

"Yes, here too," said Jonas, emphasising the last word, and with a reproachful glance at his master, added, "I am used to it, to be sure."

"Certainly," laughed Hugo. "But I am not used to your doing such things for others than myself. Who has given you the commission?"

"Herr Reinhold," was the laconic reply.

"My brother--so?" said Hugo, slowly, while a shade flitted across his features, so bright just now.

"And it is a sin the sum I am to pay for it," muttered Jonas. "Herr Reinhold understands even better than we how to throw away dollars for things which will be faded to-morrow, and we at any rate are not married, but he--"

"The bouquet is of course for my sister-in-law?" the Captain interrupted shortly. "What is there to wonder at? Do you think I shall give my wife no bouquets when I am married?"

The last remark must have been very unexpected by the sailor, as he drew himself up with a jerk, and stared at his master in the most perfect horror, but the next minute he returned reassured to his old position, saying confidently--

"We shall never marry, Herr Captain."

"I forbid all such prophetic remarks, which condemn me without further ado to perpetual celibacy," said Hugo quickly, "and why shall '*we*' never marry?"

"Because we think nothing of women," persisted Jonas.

"You have a very curious habit of always speaking in the plural," scoffed the Captain. "So I think nothing of women; I thought the contrary had often roused your ire?"

"But it never comes to marriage," said Jonas triumphantly, in a tone of unconquerable conviction, "at heart we do not think much of the whole lot. The story never goes beyond sending flowers and kissing hands, then we sail away, and they have the pleasure of looking after us. It is a very lucky thing that it is so. Women on the 'Ellida'--Heaven protect us from it!"

This characteristic account, given with unmistakable seriousness, although again in the unavoidable plural, appeared to be full of truth, as the Captain raised no objection to it. He only shrugged his shoulders laughingly, turned his back upon the sailor, and went upstairs. He found Reinhold in his own rooms, which lay in the upper story, and a single glance at his brother's face, who was walking angrily up and down, showed him that something must have happened again to-day.

"You are going out?" asked he, after greeting him, while looking at the hat and gloves lying on the table.

"Later on!" answered Reinhold, recovering himself. "In about an hour. You will stay some time?"

Hugo overlooked the last question. He stood opposite his brother, and gazed searchingly at him.

"Has there been a scene again?" he asked half-aloud.

The moody defiance, which had disappeared for a few moments from the young man's face, returned.

"To be sure. They have attempted once more to treat me like a schoolboy, who, when he has accomplished his daily appointed task, is to be watched, and made to render an account of every step he takes, even in his hours of recreation. I have made it clear to them that I am tired of their everlasting guardianship."

The Captain did not ask what step the quarrel was about; the short conversation with Jonas seemed to have explained all that sufficiently; he only said, shaking his head--"It is unfortunate that you are so completely dependent upon our uncle. If later on it end in a regular rupture between you, and you leave the business, it would become a question of existence for you--your income goes entirely with it. You, yourself, might trust wholly to your compositions, but to think they could support a family yet would be making your future very uncertain from the beginning. I had only myself to act for; you will be compelled to wait until a greater work places you in the position of being able to turn your back, with your wife and child, upon all the envy of a small provincial town."

"Impossible!" cried Reinhold almost madly. "By that time I shall have foundered ten times over, and what talent I possess with me. Endure, wait, perhaps for years? I cannot do it, it is the same thing to me as suicide. My new work is completed. If only in some degree it attain the success of the first, it would enable me to live at least a few months in Italy."

Hugo was staggered.

CHAPTER V

"You are going to Italy? Why there particularly?" asked the Captain.

"Where then?" interposed Reinhold impatiently. "Italy is the school of all art and artists. There alone could I complete the meagre, defective study to which circumstances confined me. Can you not understand that?"

"No," said the Captain, somewhat coldly. "I do not see the necessity that a beginner should go at once to the higher school. You can find opportunity enough for study here; most of our talented men have had to struggle and work for years before Italy at last crowned their work. Supposing, however, you carry out your plan, what is to become of your wife and child in the meanwhile? Do you intend to take them with you?"

"Ella?" cried the young man, in an almost contemptuous voice. "That would be the most certain method of rendering my success impossible. Do you think, that in the first step I take towards freedom, I could drag the whole chain of domestic misery with me?"

A slight frown was perceptible between Hugo's eyes--

"That sounds very hard, Reinhold," he answered.

"Is it my fault, that I am at last conscious of the truth?" growled Reinhold. "My wife cannot raise herself above the sphere of cooking and household management. It is not her fault, I know, but it is not therefore any less the misfortune of my life."

"Ella's incapacity, certainly seems settled as a sort of dogma in the family," remarked the Captain quietly. "You believe in it blindly, like the rest. Have you ever given yourself the trouble to find out if this accepted fact be really infallible?"

Reinhold shrugged his shoulders--

"I think it would be unnecessary in this case. But in none can there be a question of my taking Ella with me. Naturally she will remain with the child in her parents' house until I return."

"Until you return--and if that do not happen?"

"What do you say? What do you mean?" said the young man angrily, while a deep colour spread over his face.

Hugo crossed his arms and looked fiercely at him--

"It strikes me you are now suddenly coming forward with ready-made plans, which have certainly long been arranged, and probably well talked over. Do not deny it Reinhold! You, by yourself, would never have gone to such extremities as you do now in the disputes with my uncle, listening to no advice or representations; there is some foreign influence at work. Is it really absolutely necessary that you should go day after day to Biancona?"

Reinhold vouchsafed no reply; he turned away, and so withdrew himself from his brother's observation.

"It is talked of already in the town," continued the latter. "It cannot continue long without the report reaching here. Is it a matter of perfect indifference to you?"

"Signora Biancona is studying my new composition," said Reinhold shortly, "and I only see in her the ideal of an actress. You admired her also?"

"Admired, yes! At least in the beginning. She never attracted me. The beautiful Signora has something too vampire-like in her eyes. I fear that whoever it be, upon whom she fixes those eyes with the intention of holding him fast, will require a powerful dose of strength of will in order to remain master of himself."

At the last words he had gone to his brother's side, who now turned round slowly and looked at him.

"Have you experienced that already?" he asked, gloomily.

"I? No!" replied Hugo, with a touch of his old mocking humour. "Fortunately I am very unimpressionable as regards such-like romantic dangers, besides being sufficiently used to them. Call it frivolity--inconstancy--what you will--but a woman cannot fascinate me long or deeply; the passionate element is wanting in me. You have it only too strongly, and when you encounter anything of the sort, the danger lies close by. Take care of yourself, Reinhold!"

"Do you wish to remind me of the fetters I bear?" asked Reinhold, bitterly. "As if I did not feel them daily, hourly, and with them the powerlessness to destroy them. If I were free as you, when you tore yourself away from this bondage, all might be well; but you are right, they chained me by times, and a bridal altar is the most secure bar which can be placed before all longing for freedom--I experience it now."

They were interrupted; the servant from the house brought a message from the bookkeeper to young Herr Almbach. The latter bade the man go, and turned to his brother.

"I must go to the office for a moment. You see I am not in much danger of coming to grief by excessive romance; our ledgers, in which, probably, a couple of dollars are not properly entered, guard against that. Adieu until we meet again, Hugo!"

He went, and the Captain remained alone. He stayed a few moments as if lost in thought, while the frown on his brow became still darker; then suddenly he raised himself as with some resolve, and left the room, but not to go to the lower floor to his uncle or aunt; he went straight to the opposite apartments inhabited by his sister-in-law.

Ella was there; she sat by the window, her head was bent over some needlework, but it seemed as if this had been seized hurriedly when the door opened unexpectedly; the handkerchief thrown down hastily, and the inflamed eyelids betrayed freshly dried tears. She looked up at her brother-in-law's entrance with undisguised astonishment. It was certainly the first time he had sought her rooms; he came half-way only, and then stood still without approaching her seat.

"May the adventurer dare to come near you, Ella? or did that condemning verdict banish him entirely from your threshold?"

The young wife blushed; she turned her work about in her hands in most painful confusion.

"Herr--"

"Captain!" interrupted Hugo. "Quite right--thus do my sailors address me. Once more this name from your lips, and I shall never trouble you again with my presence. Pray Ella, listen to me to-day!" he continued determinedly, as the young wife made signs of rising. "This time I shall keep the door barred by which you always try to elude my approach; fortunately, too, there is no maid near whom you can keep by your side for some task. We are alone, and I give you my word I shall not leave this spot until I am either forgiven, or--hear the unavoidable 'Herr Captain' which will drive me away once for all."

Ella raised her eyes, and now it was plainly evident that she had wept.

"What do you care for my forgiveness?" she replied quickly. "You have wounded me least of all; I only spoke in the name of my parents and all the household."

"For them I do not care," said Hugo with the most unabashed candour, "but that I have hurt you I do regret, very much regret; it has lain like a nightmare upon me until now. I can surely do no more than beg honestly and heartily for forgiveness. Are you still angry with me, Ella?"

He put out his hand towards her. In the movement and words there lay such a warm, open kindliness and frankness, that it seemed almost impossible to refuse the petition, and Ella actually, although somewhat reluctantly, laid her hand in his.

"No," said she, simply.

"Thank God!" cried Hugo, drawing a long breath. "So at last my rights as brother-in-law are conceded. I thus take solemn possession of them."

The words were followed by the deed, as he drew forward a chair and sat down beside her. "Do you know, Ella, that since our late encounter you have interested me very much?" continued he.

"It seems one must be rude to you in order to arouse your interest," remarked Ella, almost reproachfully.

"Yes, it appears so," agreed the Captain, with perfect composure. "We 'adventurers' are a peculiar people, and require different treatment to ordinary mankind. You have taken the right course with me. Since you read me my lecture so unsparingly, I have left all the house in peace; I have behaved towards my uncle and aunt with the most perfect respect and deference, and even robbed my Indian stories of all their appalling effects, simply from fear of certain rebuking eyes. This can surely not have escaped your notice?"

Something like a half-smile crossed Ella's countenance as she asked--

"It has been very hard for you, then?"

"Very hard! Although the state of affairs in the house should have made it somewhat easier for me, they have not been of a description lately, on which one could exercise one's love of joking."

The passing gleam of merriment vanished immediately from Ella's face at this allusion; it bore an anxious, beseeching expression, as she turned to her brother-in-law.

"Yes, it is very sad with us," she said, softly, "and it becomes worse from day to day. My parents are so hard, and Reinhold so irritated, so furious at every occurrence. Oh, my God, can you do nothing with him?"

"I?" asked Hugo, seriously, "I might put that question to you, his wife."

Ella shook her head in inconsolable resignation. "No one listens to me, and Reinhold less than any one. He thinks I understand nothing about it all--he would repulse me roughly."

Hugo looked sorrowfully at the young wife, who confessed openly that she was quite wanting in power and influence over her husband, and that she was not permitted to share his longings and strivings in the least.

"And yet something must be done," said he decidedly. "Reinhold irritates himself in this struggle; he suffers tremendously under it, and makes others suffer too. You had been crying, Ella, as I entered, and in the last few weeks not a day has passed without my seeing this red appearance about your eyes. No, do not turn aside so timidly! Surely the brother may be allowed to speak freely, and you shall see that I do more than talk nonsense. I repeat it; something must be done--done by you. Reinhold's artistic career depends upon it, his whole future; and in the struggle his wife must stand at his side, otherwise others might do it instead, and that would be dangerous."

Ella looked at him with a mixture of astonishment and alarm. For the first time in her life she was called upon to take a side openly, and some result was looked for depending upon her interference. What could be meant by "others" who might take her place? Her face showed plainly that she had not the slightest suspicion of anything.

Hugo saw this, and yet had not the courage to go any farther; as going farther meant planting the first suspicion in the mind of the so-far quite unconscious wife--being his brother's betrayer--and unavoidably calling forth a catastrophe, of whose necessity he was nevertheless convinced. But the young Captain's whole nature rebelled against the painful task; he sat there undecided, when chance came to his help. Some one knocked at the door, and immediately Jonas entered, carrying a large bouquet of flowers.

The sailor was surely more prudent when he executed such commissions for his master. He knew from experience, that the latter's offerings of flowers, although received with pleasure by the young ladies, were not always treated the same by their fathers and protectors, and although with possible secret annoyance, he always took care to go to the right address. But this time Hugo's casual remark that the flowers were intended for his sister-in-law, caused the mistake. Jonas never doubted that the Captain's remark, meant merely to shield his brother, was made in earnest; he therefore went straight to the young Frau Almbach, and presented the flowers to her, with the words--

"I cannot find Herr Reinhold anywhere in the house, so had better deliver the flowers here at once."

Ella looked down in surprise at the beautiful bouquet which, arranged with as much skill as taste, showed a selection of the most perfect flowers.

"From whom are the flowers?" asked she.

"From the garden," answered Jonas. "Herr Reinhold ordered them, and I have brought them; but as I cannot find him--"

"That will do. You can go," broke in Hugo, as he stepped quickly to his sister-in-law's side, and put his hand on her arm as if to stop her. A sign gave more stress to his order, and Jonas rolled away, but could not help wondering that the young Frau Almbach received her husband's attention in so peculiar a manner. She had started suddenly, as if she had been seized with a pain at her heart, and become ashen white. But the Captain stood there with knitted brows, and an expression on his face as if he should have liked best to throw the expensive flowers out of the window. Fortunately, Jonas was too phlegmatic to trouble himself much about the state of affairs in the Almbachs' house; owing to the warlike footing on which he stood to the servants he learned but little about it; so, after wondering slightly, he gave it up, and being satisfied he had executed his orders conscientiously, troubled himself no more about the giver of them.

Deep silence reigned a few seconds in the room. Ella still held the bouquet convulsively in her hand, but her usually quiet, listless countenance, with its vacant, almost stupid expression, had changed curiously. Now every feature was dilated as if in agonising pain, and her eyes remained fixed and immovable upon the gay, blooming beauty, even when she turned to her brother-in-law.

"Reinhold gave the order?" she asked, as if striving for breath, "then the flowers only came by mistake to me!"

"Why then," said Hugo, with a vain attempt to soothe her, "Reinhold ordered the flowers; well, surely they are for you?"

"For me?" Her voice sounded full of pain. "I have never yet received flowers from him; these are certainly not intended for me."

Hugo saw he could not hesitate any more; chance had decided for him; now he must obey fate's signal. "You are right, Ella," he replied firmly, "and it would be useless and dangerous to deceive you any longer. Reinhold did not say for whom the flowers were, but I know that this evening they will be in Signora Biancona's hands."

Ella shivered, and the bouquet fell to the ground. "Signora Biancona," repeated she, in a dull tone.

"The actress who sang his first song in public," continued the Captain, impressively, "for whom, also, his new composition is intended; to whom he goes daily; who enters into all his thoughts and feelings. You know nothing of it as yet, I see in your face, but you must learn it now, before it is too late."

The young wife made no reply; her face was as colourless as the white blossoms which formed the outer circle of the bouquet; silently she stooped, picked it up, and laid it on the table, but no sound, no response came from her lips. Hugo waited for one in vain.

"Do you believe the cruelty of disclosing that which one always hides from every wife has given me any pleasure?" asked he, with suppressed emotion. "Do you think I could not, by some pretence, have covered the man's stupidity, and given myself out as the sender of the unlucky flowers? If I do not act thus, if I discover the whole truth unsparingly, I do it because the danger has become extreme--because only you can still save him; and this you must see clearly. Signora Biancona is about to return to her home, and Reinhold explained to me just now that he must and will continue his studies in Italy. Do you comprehend the connection?"

Ella started. Now, for the first time, a desperate fear broke through the stolid calm of her nature.

"No, no!" she cried, as if beside herself, "He cannot! he *dare* not. We are married!"

"He dare not?" repeated Hugo. "You know men but little, and your own husband least of all. Do not trust too much to the right which the Church gave you; even this power has its limits, and I fear Reinhold already stands beyond them. To be sure, you have no conception of that burning fiendish passion, which enchains and makes a man powerless--so surrounds him with its bonds, that for its sake he forgets and sacrifices everything. Signora Biancona is one of those demonlike natures which can inspire such passions, and here she is connected with everything which makes up Reinhold's life--with music, art and imagination. Nor Church nor marriage can protect, if the wife cannot protect herself. You are wife, and mother of his child. Perhaps he will listen to your voice, when he will to nothing else." The young wife's heavily-drawn breath showed how much she suffered, and two tears, the first, rolled slowly down her cheeks as she replied, almost inaudibly, "I will try it."

Hugo came close to her side. "I know I have thrown a lighted brand into the family to-day, which will, perhaps, destroy the last remains of peace," he said, earnestly. "Hundreds of wives would now rush despairingly to their parents, so as, with them or alone, to call their husbands to account, and cause a scene which would break the last bond, and drive him irretrievably from the house. You will not do this, Ella; I know it, therefore I dared do with you what I should not have ventured on so easily with any other woman. What you may say to Reinhold--what you may insist upon, rests with yourself; but do not let him leave you now; do not let him go to Italy!"

He ceased, and seemed to expect an answer--in vain; Ella sat there, her face buried in her hands. She hardly moved as he said good-bye to her. The young Captain saw that she must overcome the blow alone, so he went.

When, half-an-hour later, Reinhold returned from the office, he saw the bouquet of roses lying on the writing-table in his own room, and took it up under the firm impression that Jonas had put it there. In the meanwhile Ella sat in her child's room and waited, not for a farewell from her husband, she had not been used to such tendernesses ever since her marriage; but she knew he never left the house without first going to see his boy. The wife felt only too well that she herself was nothing to her husband, that her only value for him lay in the child; she felt that the love for his child was the only point by which she could approach his heart, and therefore she waited here for him in order to hold the terribly difficult and painful interview. He must surely come; but to-day she had to wait in vain. Reinhold did not come. For the first time he forgot the farewell kiss on his child's brow--forgot the last and only bond which chained him to his home. In his heart there was only room now for one thought, and that was Beatrice Biancona.

The opera was over. A stream of people flowed out of the theatre, dispersing in all directions, and carriages rolled by on every side to take up their respective owners. The house had been filled to overflowing, as the Italian Opera Company had given their farewell performance, and all H---- had tried to show the singers, especially the *prima donna*, how much charmed it was with their efforts, and how sorry it was to lose them now the hour of parting had arrived. The stairs and corridors were still crowded; below in the vestibule people were closely packed, and at the places of egress the numbers increased to an uncomfortable, almost dangerous degree.

"It is almost impossible to get through," said Doctor Welding, who, with another gentleman, descended the stairs. "One's life is imperilled in the crush below. Rather let us wait until the rush is over!"

His companion agreed, and both stepped aside into one of the deep, dark niches in the corridor, where a lady had already taken shelter. Her dress, although simple, betokened that she belonged to the upper classes; she had drawn her veil closely over her face, and appeared to avoid the crowd, also to feel quite strange in the theatre, from the manner in which she pressed herself with evident nervousness firmly against the wall, when the two gentlemen approached, and, without paying any attention to her, resumed their interrupted conversation.

"I prophesied it from the commencement that this Almbach would make a great sensation," said Welding; "his second composition surpasses his first in every respect; and the first was great enough for a beginner. I should think he might be satisfied with its reception this time; it was, if possible, more enthusiastic. Certainly, every one has not the luck to find a Biancona for his works, and to inspire her for them, so that she exerts her utmost power. It was altogether her idea to sing this newest song of Almbach's as introduction to the last act of the opera, to-day, too, at her farewell; when applause was a matter of course, she made sure, by those means, of success at once."

"Well, I don't think he is wanting in gratitude," scoffed the other gentleman. "People say all sorts of things. So much is certain, all her circle of adorers is furious at this interloper, who hardly appears before he is on the high road to be sole ruler. The affair, besides, seems rather serious and highly romantic, and I am really anxious to see what will be the end of it, when Biancona departs."

The Doctor buttoned his overcoat quietly--

"That is not difficult to guess; an elopement of the first order."

"You think he will elope with her?" asked the other incredulously.

"He with her? That would be objectless. Biancona is perfectly free to decide what she likes, as to the choice of her residence. But she with him; that would be more like the case--the fetters are on his side."

"To be sure, he is married," rejoined his companion. "Poor woman! Do you know her personally?"

"No," said Welding, indifferently; "but from Herr Consul Erlau's description, I can form a truly correct picture of her. Contracted ideas, passive, unimportant in the highest degree, quite given up to the kitchen and household affairs--just the woman in fact to drive a genial, fiery-headed fellow like Almbach to a desperate step; and as it is a Biancona who is set up against her, this step will not have to be waited for very long. Perhaps it would be fortunate for Almbach if he were torn suddenly out of these confined surroundings, and thrown on to the path of life, but certainly the little family peace there is would be entirely ruined. The usual fate of such early marriages, in which the wife cannot in the smallest degree raise herself to her husband's importance."

At these last words he turned round somewhat astonished; involuntarily the lady behind them had made a passionate movement, but at the same moment as the Doctor was about to observe her more narrowly, a side door was opened, and Reinhold Almbach appeared, accompanied by Hugo, the conductor, and several other gentlemen.

Reinhold here was quite a different being from what he was at home. The gloom which always rested on his features there, the reserve which made him so often unapproachable, seemed thrown off with one accord; he beamed with excitement, success, and triumph. His brow was raised freely and proudly, his dark eyes flashed with conscious victory, and his whole manner breathed forth passionate satisfaction, as he turned to his companions.

"I thank you, gentlemen. You are very kind, but you will excuse me if I retire from these flattering acknowledgments. The Signora wishes for my company at the entertainment, where the members of the opera assemble once more as a farewell meeting. You will understand, I must obey this command before all others."

The gentlemen seemed to understand it perfectly, and also to regret they had not to obey a similar command, when Doctor Welding joined the group.

"I congratulate you," he said, giving his hand to the young composer. "That was a great, and what is more, a merited success."

Reinhold smiled. Praise from the lips of a critic usually so exacting was not indifferent to him.

"You see, Herr Doctor, I have to appear at last before your judgment seat," replied he pleasantly. "Herr Consul Erlau was unfortunately wrong when he considered me quite safe from any such danger."

"None should be considered happy before the end," remarked the Doctor laconically. "Why do you rush so headlong into danger, and turn your back upon the noble merchant's position? Is it true we are to lose you with Signora Biancona? Shall you take flight to the south at the same time?"

"To Italy, yes!" said Reinhold positively. "It has been my plan for long. This evening has decided it, but now--excuse me gentlemen, I cannot possibly allow the Signora to wait."

He bowed and left them, accompanied by his brother. The usually not quite silent Captain had observed a remarkable reticence during the conversation. He started slightly, when at Welding's approach the niche was disclosed in which the woman's dark figure was pressed back in the shadow of the wall, as if not wishing to be seen on any account, and no one else did see her, at least no one took any notice of her; she could not leave her place of refuge without passing the group, which kept its place after the departure of the brothers. The gentlemen all knew one another, and took advantage of this meeting to exchange their opinions about the young composer, Signora Biancona, and the suspected state of affairs between the two. The latter especially was subjected to a tolerably merciless criticism. The scoffing, witty, and malicious remarks fell thick as hail, and some time elapsed before the group separated at last. Now that the corridor was quite empty, the lady in the recess raised herself and prepared to depart, but she tottered at the first few steps, and seized the banisters of the staircase as if about to fall, when a powerful arm supported, and held her up.

CHAPTER VI

"Come into the fresh air, Ella!" said Hugo, standing suddenly beside her. "That was torture of the rack."

He drew her hand within his arm, and led her down by the nearest way into the street. Only here, in the cool, sharp night air did Ella appear to regain consciousness; she threw back her veil and drew a long breath, as if she had been nearly suffocated.

"If I had dreamed that my warning would have brought you here, I should have withheld it." continued Hugo, reproachfully. "Ella, for heaven's sake, what an unfortunate idea!"

The young wife drew her hand away from his arm. The reproach seemed to pain her.

"I wanted to see her for once," replied she softly.

"Without being seen yourself?" added the Captain. "I knew that the moment I recognised you, therefore I said nothing to Reinhold, but I felt as if standing on hot coals here below, while the criticising group above was holding forth before your place of refuge, and giving free course to their amiable remarks and opinions. I can fancy pretty well what you had to listen to."

During the last words he had hailed a cabman, told the street and number of house, and helped his sister-in-law into the carriage; but as he showed signs of taking a seat beside her, she declined his doing so, quietly but firmly.

"Thanks, I shall go alone."

"On no account!" cried Hugo, almost excitedly. "You are much agitated, almost fainting; it would be unpardonable to leave you alone in this state."

"You are not responsible for what becomes of me," said Ella, with uncontrolled bitterness, "and to others--it does not matter. Let me drive home alone, Hugo, I beseech you."

Her eyes looked at him entreatingly through their veil of tears. The Captain did not say another word; he shut the door obediently, and stepped back; but he watched the carriage as it rolled away until it was out of sight.

It was long past midnight when Reinhold returned, and, without entering his house, he went at once to his garden room. The house and outbuildings lay still and dark; nothing was moving around, all who lived and worked here were accustomed to be occupied in the daytime, and required the night for undisturbed repose. It was fortunate that the garden-house lay so distant and isolated, otherwise his companions and neighbours would have been much less patient with the young composer, who could not refrain, however late he might return home, from always seeking his piano, and often morning's dawn surprised him at his musical phantasies.

It was a quiet, moonlight, but sharp raw northern spring night. In the dawning light, the walls and gables which enclosed the garden looked even more gloomy and prison-like than by day; the canal appeared darker in the pale moon's rays, which trembled over it, and the bare leafless trees and shrubs seemed to tremble and shudder in the cold night wind, which passed mercilessly over them. It was already April, and yet the first buds were hardly to be seen. "This miserable spring, with its tardy growth and bloom, its dreary rainy days and cold winds!" Reinhold had heard these words spoken a few hours since, and then such a glowing description followed of endless spring, which blossoms forth as by magic in the gardens of the south, those sunny days, with ever blue sky, and the thousandfold glorious colours of the earth; the moonlight nights full of orange perfume and notes of song. The young man must indeed have head and heart still full of this picture; he looked more contemptuously than usual on the poor bare surroundings, and impatiently pushed aside a branch of elderberry whose newly opening brown buds touched his forehead. He had no more feeling for the gifts of this miserable spring, and no more pleasure in growing and living as miserably as these blossoms, ever fighting with frost and wind. Out into freedom, that was the only thought which now filled his mind.

Reinhold opened the door of the garden room and started back with sudden alarm. A few seconds elapsed before he recognised his wife in the figure leaning against the piano standing out clearly in the moonlight as it fell through the window.

"Is it you, Ella?" he cried at last, entering quickly. "What is it? What has happened?"

She made a movement of denial. "Nothing, I was only waiting for you."

"Here? and at this hour?" asked Reinhold, extremely distantly. "What has entered your head?"

"I hardly ever see you now," was the soft response, "at least only at table in my parents' presence, and I wished to speak to you alone."

She had lighted the lamp at these words, and placed it upon the table. She still wore the dark silk dress which she had on at the theatre this evening; it was certainly plain and unornamented, but not so coarse and unbecoming as her usual house dress. Also her never failing cap had disappeared, and now, that it was missing, could be seen for the first time what a singular wealth was hidden beneath it. The fair hair, of which at other times only a narrow strip was visible, could hardly be confined in the heavy plaits which showed themselves in all their splendid abundance; but this natural ornament, which any other woman would have displayed, was in her case hidden carefully day after day, until chance disclosed it, and yet it appeared to give her head quite a different mould.

As usual, Reinhold had no eyes for it; he hardly looked at his young wife, and only listened slightly and abstractedly to her words. There was not even the slightest trace of reproach in them, but he must have felt something of the sort lay there as he said impatiently--

"You know I am occupied on all possible sides. My new composition which was completed a few weeks since, was brought out publicly to-night for the first time--"

"I know it," interrupted Ella. "I was in the theatre."

Reinhold seemed taken aback. "You were in the theatre?" asked he quickly and sharply. "With whom? At whose instigation?"

"I was there alone--I wished--" she stopped, and continued hesitatingly; "I too wished to hear your music for once, of which all the world speaks and I alone do not know."

Her husband was silent and looked enquiringly at her. The young wife did not understand the art of deceiving, and an untruth would not pass her lips. She stood before him, deadly pale, trembling in all her limbs; no especially keen sight was required to guess the truth, and Reinhold did so at once.

"And only for this reason you went?" said he slowly at last. "Will you deceive me with this excuse, or yourself, perhaps? I see the report has found its way to you already! You wished to see with your own eyes, naturally. How could I think it would be spared me and you?"

Ella looked up. There was again the darkly lowering brow she was always accustomed to in her husband, the look of gloomy melancholy, the expression of defiant, suppressed suffering, no longer a breath of that beaming triumph which had lighted up his features a few hours before--that was when away, far from his own people; only the shadow remained for home.

"Why do you not answer?" he began afresh. "Do you think I should be coward enough to deny the truth? If I have been silent towards you so far, it was done to spare you; now that you know it, I will render account. You have been told of the young actress, to whom I owe the first incitement to work, my first success, and to-day's triumph. God knows how the connection between us has been represented to you, and naturally you look upon it as a crime worthy of death."

"No, but as a misfortune."

The tone of these words would surely have disarmed any one; even Reinhold's irritation could not resist it. He came nearer to her and took her hand.

"Poor child!" said he, pitifully. "It certainly was no happiness what your father's will decided for you. You, more than any other, required a husband who would work and strive from day to day in the quiet routine of daily life without even having a wish to step beyond it, and fate has chained you to a man whom it draws powerfully to another course. You are right; that is a misfortune for us both."

"That is to say, I am one for you," added the young wife, sadly. "She will, perhaps, know better how to bring you happiness."

Reinhold let her hand fall and stepped back. "You are mistaken," he replied, almost rudely, "and quite misconstrue the connection between Signora Biancona and myself. It has been purely ideal from the beginning, and is so still at this moment. Whoever told you differently is a liar."

At the first words, Ella seemed to breathe more easily, but at the following her heart contracted as if with cramp. She knew her husband was incapable of speaking a falsehood, least of all at such a moment, and he told her the connection was spiritual. That it was so still she did not doubt, but how long would it be so? This evening, in the theatre, she had seen the flash of those demon-like eyes, which nothing could resist; had seen how that woman, in her part, had run through the whole scale of feelings to the greatest passion; how this passion carried away the audience to a perfect storm of approbation; and she could easily tell herself that if it had pleased the Italian so far only to be the gracious goddess whose hand had led the young composer into the realms of art, the hour was sure to come in which she would wish to be more to him.

"I love Beatrice," continued Reinhold, with a cruelty of which he seemed to have no real conception; "but this love does not injure nor wound any of your rights. It only concerns music, as whose embodied genius she met me, concerns the best and highest in my life, the ideal--"

"And what is left for your wife, then?" interrupted Ella.

He remained silent, struck dumb. This question, simple as it was, sounded nevertheless peculiar from the lips of his wife, deemed so stupid. It was a matter of course, that she should be satisfied with what still remained--the name she bore and the child, whose mother she was. Strange to say, she did not appear inclined to understand this, and Reinhold became quite silent at the quiet but yet annihilating reproach of the question.

The wife rested her hand on the piano. She was visibly fighting with the fear she had always cherished for her husband, whose mental superiority she felt deeply, without, at the same time, ever venturing on an attempt to raise herself to him. In the knowledge that he stood so high above her, she had ever placed herself completely under him, without ever attaining anything by it excepting toleration, which almost amounted to contempt.

Now that he loved another, the toleration ceased; the contempt remained--she felt that plainly in his confession, which he made so quietly, so positively; his love for the beautiful singer "neither injured nor wounded any of her rights." She had indeed no right to his spiritual life. And she should keep firm hold of that man now, when the love of a beautiful, universally admired actress, when the magical charm of Italy, when a future full of renown and glory beckoned to him, she, who had nothing to give excepting herself--Ella was conscious for the first time of the impossibility of the task which had been appointed to her.

"I know you have never belonged to us, never loved any of us," she said, with quiet resignation. "I have always felt it; it has only become clear to me since I was your wife, and then it was too late. But I am it now, and if you forsake me and the child, you will give us up for the sake of another."

"Who says so?" cried Reinhold, with anger, which exonerated him from the suspicion that such a thought had really entered his mind. "Forsake? Give up you and the child? Never!"

The young wife fixed her eyes enquiringly upon him, as if she did not understand him.

"But you said just now you loved Beatrice Biancona?"

"Yes, but--"

"But! Then you must choose between her and us."

"You suddenly develope most unusual determination," cried Reinhold, roused. "I must? And if I will not do it? If I consider this ideal artist love quite compatible with my duties, if--"

"If you follow her to Italy," completed Ella.

"Then you know that already?" cried the young man, passionately. "You seem to be so perfectly informed, that it only remains for me to confirm the news others have been so kind as to tell you. It is certainly my intention to continue my studies in Italy, and if I should meet Signora Biancona there--if her vicinity give me fresh inspiration to compose--her hand open me the door to the world of art, I shall not be fool enough to reject all this, just because it is my fate to possess a--wife!"

Ella shuddered at the unsparing hardness of the last words.

"Are you so ashamed of your wife?" she asked, softly.

"Ella, I beg you--"

"Are you so ashamed of me?" repeated the poor wife, apparently calmly; but there was a strange, nervous, trembling inflection in her voice. Reinhold turned away.

"Do not be childish, Ella," he replied, impatiently. "Do you think it is good or elevating for a man, when he returns home after his first success, there to find complaints, reproaches, in short, all the wretched prose of domestic life? So far you have spared me it, and should do the same in future. Otherwise you might discover that I am not the patient sort of husband who would allow such scenes to take place without resistance."

Only a single glance at the young wife was required to recognise the boundless injustice of this reproach. She stood there, not like the accuser, but like the condemned; indeed she felt that in this hour the verdict was spoken upon her marriage and her life.

"I know well that I have never been anything to you," said she, with trembling voice, "never could be anything to you, and if I only were concerned, I would let you go without a word, without a petition. But the child is still between us, and therefore"--she stopped a moment, and breathed heavily----"therefore you can comprehend that the mother should pray once more for you to remain with us."

The petition came out shyly, hesitatingly; in it could be heard the effort it cost her to make it to the husband, in whose heart no chord throbbed for her, and yet in the last words there rang such a touching, frightened entreaty, that his ear could not remain quite deaf. He turned to her again.

"I cannot stay, Ella," he replied, more mildly than before, but still with cool decision. "My future depends on it. You cannot conceive what lies in that word for me. You cannot accompany me with the child. Besides this being quite impossible in a tour undertaken for study, you would soon be very miserable in a foreign country whose language you do not understand, in circumstances and surroundings for which you are quite unsuited. You must, indeed, now accustom yourself to measure me and my life with another measure than that of narrow-minded prejudice and middle-class contracted ideas. You can stay here with the little one, under your parents' protection; at latest I shall return in a year. You must resign yourself to this separation."

He spoke calmly, even pleasantly; but every word was an icy rejection, an impatient shaking off of the irksome bond. Hugo was right; he lay already too firmly under the influence of his passion to listen to any other voice--it was too late. A cold, pitiless, "You must resign yourself," was the only answer to that touching prayer.

Ella drew herself up with a determination at other times quite foreign to her, and there was also a strange sound in her voice; there lay in it something of the pride of a wife, who, trampled upon and kept down for years, at last revolts when extremities are resorted to.

"To the separation, yes," replied she, firmly. "I am powerless against it. But not to your return, Reinhold. If you go now, go with her, notwithstanding my prayers, notwithstanding our child, so do it. But then, go for ever!"

"Will you make conditions?" roared Reinhold, passionately. "Have I not borne the yoke which your father's so-called kindness forced upon me for years, which embittered my childhood, destroyed my youth, and now, at the threshold of man's estate, compels me to conquer, only by means of endless struggles, what every one requires as his natural right, free decision for himself? You all have kept me apart from everything that by others is called freedom and happiness; have bound me to a hated sphere in life with all possible fetters, and now think yourselves sure of your property. But at last the hour has come for me when it begins to dawn, and if it penetrates like lightning to my soul, and shows in flaming clearness the goal, and the reward at the goal, then one awakes out of the dream of long years, and finds oneself--in chains."

It was an outbreak of the wildest passion, most burning hatred, which welled forth without restraint, without asking if it were poured over the guilty or the innocent. That is the horrible fiendishness of passion, that it turns its hatred against everything which it encounters, even if this hatred meet the nearest, most sacred--if it even meet bonds voluntarily made.

A long pause, still as death, followed. Reinhold, overpowered by excitement, had thrown himself on a seat and covered his eyes with his hands. Ella still stood on the same spot as before; she did not speak or move; even the tremor which, during the conversation, had so often passed through her, had ceased. Thus passed a few moments, until at last she approached her husband slowly.

"You will leave me the child, though?" said she, with quivering lips. "To you it would only be a burden in your new life, and I have nothing else in the world."

Reinhold looked up, and then sprang suddenly from his seat. It was not the words which moved him so strangely, not the deadly, fixed calm of her face; it was the look which was so unexpectedly and astoundingly unveiled before him as before his brother. For the first time he saw in his wife's face "the beautiful fairy-tale blue eyes" which he had so often admired in his boy, without ever asking whence they came; and these eyes, large and full, were now directed towards him. No tear stood in them, neither any more beseeching; but an expression for which he never gave Ella credit, an expression before which his eyes sank to the ground.

"Ella," said he, uncertainly, "if I was too furious--What is it, Ella?"

He tried to take her hand; she drew it back.

"Nothing. When do you intend leaving?"

"I do not know," answered Reinhold, more and more struck. "In a few days--or weeks--there is no hurry."

"I will inform my parents. Good-night." She turned to go. He made a hasty step after her as if to detain her. Ella remained.

"You have misunderstood me."

The young wife drew herself up firmly and proudly. She appeared all at once to have become a different person. This tone and carriage, Ella Almbach had never known.

"The 'fetters' shall not press upon you any longer, Reinhold. You can attain your object unhindered, and your--prize. Good-night."

She opened the door quickly and went out. The moonlight fell brightly on the slight figure in the darkness, upon the sad pale face and the blond plaits. In the next moment she had disappeared. Reinhold stood alone.

"This house is miserable now," said the old bookkeeper in the office, as he put his pen behind his ear, and closed the account book. "The young master away for three days without giving any signs of his being alive, without enquiring for wife or child. The Herr Captain does not set his foot across the threshold; the principal goes about in such a rage that one hardly dares to go near him; and young Frau Almbach looks so wretched that one's heart aches to see her. Heaven knows how this unhappy story will end."

"But how, then, did this disturbance come so suddenly?" asked the head clerk, who also--it was the hour for closing the office--put his writing aside and shut his desk.

The bookkeeper shrugged his shoulders. "Suddenly? I do not believe it was unexpected by any of us. It has been smouldering in the family for weeks and months; only the spark was wanting in all this inflammable matter, and it came at last. Frau Almbach brought the news home from some lady's party, and thus her husband learned what half the town knew already, and what no one hears willingly, of his son-in-law. You know our chief, and how he always looked upon all this artist business with dislike; how he fought against it--and now this discovery! He sent for the young master, and then there was such a scene--I heard part of it in the next room. If Herr Reinhold had only behaved sensibly and given in in this case when he really was not innocent, perhaps the affair might have been set aside, instead of which he put on his most obstinate manner, told his father-in-law to his face that he would not remain a merchant, would go to Italy, would become a musician; he had endured the slavery here long enough, and much more of the same kind. The chief could not contain himself for rage; he forbade, threatened, insulted at last, and then, of course, came the end. The young master broke out so wildly that I thought something would happen. He stamped his foot like a madman, and cried--'And if the whole world set itself in opposition, it will still be. I will not be domineered over anyhow, nor allow my thoughts and feelings to be prescribed for me.' And it went on in this tone. An hour later he stormed out of the house, and has not let himself be heard of since. God protect everyone from such family scenes."

The old gentleman laid his pen aside, left his seat, and wished the others good-night, while he prepared to leave the office. He had hardly gone a few steps along the passage when he met Herr Almbach, who turned in quickly from the street. The bookkeeper struck his hands together in joyful alarm.

"Thank God that you, at least, are to be seen again, Herr Captain," he cried. "We are indeed wretched in this house."

"Is the barometer still pointing to stormy?" asked Hugo, with a glance at the upper story.

The bookkeeper sighed. "Stormy! Perhaps you will bring us sunshine."

"Hardly," said Hugo, seriously. "At this moment I am seeking Frau Almbach. Is she at home?"

"Your aunt is out with the chief," said the former.

"Not she. I mean my sister-in-law."

"The young mistress? Oh dear, we have not seen her for three days. She is sure to be upstairs in the nursery. She hardly leaves the little one for a moment now."

"I will seek her," said Hugo, as with a rapid adieu he hastened upstairs. "Good-evening."

The bookkeeper looked after him, shaking his head. He was not used to the young Captain's passing him without some joke, some chaff; and he had also remarked the cloud which to-day lay on the young man's usually cheerful brow. He shook his head once more, and repeated his former sigh, "God knows how the affair will end."

In the meanwhile Hugo had reached his sister-in-law's apartments.

"It is I, Ella," he said, entering. "Have I startled you?"

The young wife was alone; she sat by her boy's little bed. The rapid, youthful steps outside, and the quick opening of the door, might well have deceived her as to the comer. She had surely expected another. Her painful start and the colour in her face, which suddenly gave way to intense pallor, as she recognised her brother-in-law, showed this.

"My uncle carries his injustice so far as to forbid me the house also," continued the latter, as he came nearer. "He persists in thinking I had some share in this unhappy breach. I hope, Ella, that you exonerate me from it."

She hardly listened to the last words. "You bring me news from Reinhold?" asked she quickly, with fleeting breath. "Where is he?"

"You surely did not expect that he would come himself," said the Captain, evasively. "Whatever blame may be due to him in the whole affair, the behaviour on my uncle's part was such that every one would have rebelled against it. On this point I stand on his side, and understand thoroughly that he went with the intention not to return. I should have done the same."

"It was a terrible scene," replied Ella, with difficulty keeping back the tears which were gushing out. "My parents learned elsewhere what I would have hidden at any cost, and Reinhold was awful in his wild rage. He left us, but he might have let me receive one word at least, during the three days, through you. He is surely with you?"

"No," replied Hugo, shortly, almost roughly.

"No," repeated Ella, "he is not with you? I took it as a matter of course that he would be there."

The Captain looked down. "He came to me, and with the intention of remaining, but a difference arose between us about it. Reinhold is unboundedly passionate when a certain point is touched upon; I could and would not hide my feelings about it, and we quarrelled for the first time in our lives. He thereupon refused to be friends; I have only seen him again this morning."

Ella did not reply. She did not even ask what was the cause of the quarrel; she felt only too well that in her brother-in-law, esteemed so frivolous, mischievous, and heartless, she possessed the most energetic protector of her rights.

"I have tried my utmost once more," said he, coming close beside her, "although I knew it would be in vain. But you, Ella, could you not keep him?"

"No," replied the young wife, "I could not, and at last I would not."

Instead of any response, Hugo pointed to the sleeping babe; Ella shook her head violently.

"For his sake I conquered myself, and begged the husband, who wished to tear himself away from me at any price, to remain. I was repulsed; he let me feel what a fetter I am to him--he may then go free."

Hugo's glance rested enquiringly on her countenance, that again showed the energetic expression which was once so foreign to her features. Slowly he drew forth a note.

"If then you are prepared, I have a few lines to bring you from Reinhold. He gave me them two or three hours since."

The wife started. The firmness she had just shown could not continue when she saw her husband's handwriting on the envelope; only his handwriting, while with mortal agony she had clung to the hope that he would come himself, if it had merely been to say farewell. With trembling hand she took the letter and opened it; it contained only a few lines--

"You witnessed the scene between your father and myself, and will therefore comprehend that I do not enter his house again. That scene has changed nothing in my decision. It only hastens my departure, as the want of tact on your parents' part has given the affair a publicity which does not make it appear desirable for me to remain an hour longer in H---- than is absolutely necessary. I cannot bid you and the child good-bye personally, as I shall not set foot again across a threshold from which I was driven in such a manner. It is not my fault if a separation, which I was resolved to obtain for a time, now becomes a lengthened one that is brought about by a violent quarrel. It was you who made the condition, that I should either remain or go for ever. Well, then, I go! Perhaps it will be better for us both. Farewell!"

CHAPTER VII

The Captain must have known what the letter contained, as he stood close by Ella's side, apparently ready to support her, as in the theatre; but this time she betrayed no weakness. She looked silently down at the icy words of farewell with which her husband freed himself from wife and child. With what haste had he seized the excuse which her father's harshness and her own words offered him; with what relief had he shaken off the irksome bonds! This blow did not fall unexpectedly now. Since that last interview she knew her fate.

"He is gone already?" asked she, without raising her eyes from the letter, which she still held in her hand.

"An hour ago."

"And with her?"

Hugo was silent; he could not say "No" to this question. Ella rose, apparently calm, but she leaned heavily on the boy's bed.

"I knew it. And now--leave me alone, I implore you!"

The Captain hesitated. "I came, also, to bid you adieu," replied he. "My departure was decided without this, and now, in my brother's absence, nothing keeps me. I shall make no attempt to remove my uncle's absurd prejudice against me, but I should like to take a word of farewell from you, Ella, away with me. Will you refuse it me?"

The young woman raised her eyes slowly; they met his, and as if following an involuntary impulse, held out both hands to him--

"I thank you, Hugo, farewell!"

With a quick movement he caught her hands in his--

"I have ever only been able to bring you pain," he said softly. "By me came the first news which utterly destroyed your peace; it came too late, and to-day it was again my hand which brought you the last. But if I pained you, Ella, must pain you--my God, it has not been easy for me."

His lips rested for a moment on her hand, then he let it fall, and left the room quickly; a few moments later he was in the open air.

It was a raw, regular northern spring evening. The rain fell steadily; mist hung heavily and densely in the streets; even the lamp light only shone dimly red in the grey atmosphere. The rolling train bore Reinhold Almbach away in this fog to the south, where fame and love, where his future beckoned brightly to him; and in the same hour his young wife lay at home on her knees by her child's cradle, pressing her head in the pillow to smother the cry of despair, which now, that she knew herself to be alone, broke forth at last. He had not come once to say adieu; he had not one kind last word for her; not one farewell kiss for his child. They were both forsaken, given up--probably forgotten already.

The blazing glory of the sunset seemed to bathe heaven and earth in a sea of fire, and illumination. All the wonderful colouring of the south lighted up the western horizon, and the flood of light poured itself far away over the town, with its cupolas, towers, and palaces. It was an incomparable panorama stretching around the villa, which lay outside the town on a slight elevation visible from afar, with its terrace and colonnades, surrounded by the lower lying gardens, in which the most luxuriant southern vegetation displayed itself. There sombre cypresses raised their gloomy heads; pines waved in the gentle evening wind; white marble statues peeped forth through laurel and myrtle bushes; the waters from the fountains rippled and fell on the carpet of turf; and thousands of flowers sent forth their intoxicating sweet perfume--everywhere beauty and art, scent and flowers, light and dazzling colours.

A numerous party was assembled on the terrace and in the adjoining parts of the park, preferring the enjoyment of this beautiful evening, and the wonderful view outside, to remaining in the rooms. It seemed principally to consist of the aristocracy, yet many a figure might be seen there which undoubtedly betrayed the artist, and here and there appeared the dark habit of a priest near the light toilettes of the ladies or brilliant uniforms. The most different elements seemed to be united here. They walked, chatted, and sat or stood together in unconstrained groups.

In one of these groups, which had gathered at the foot of a terrace close to the great fountain, the conversation was conducted with unusual vivacity; it must be about some subject of general interest. The few words and names mentioned appeared to rouse the attention of one of the guests, and he, coming from the terrace, passed close by the group. He was clearly a stranger, as was denoted by his light brown hair, eyes, and indeed his whole face, which, although tanned by sun and air, still did not show the dark colouring of the southerner. The uniform of a captain set off his strong manly figure very advantageously, and in his bearing and movements was a happy combination of the free, somewhat easy manner of a sailor with the forms of good society. He stopped near the gentlemen who were talking so eagerly, and listened to their conversation with evident interest.

"This new opera is, and will be the chief event of the season," said an officer in the uniform of the carbineers, "and therefore I do not understand how it can be so easily postponed. The performance is already arranged, the rehearsals have begun, all preparations are nearly finished, when suddenly everything is interrupted, and the whole performance postponed until the autumn, and all this without any apparent reason."

"The reason lies alone in the sovereign pleasure of Signor Rinaldo," replied another gentleman, in a somewhat ill-natured tone. "He is accustomed to treat the opera and public according to his humour and fancy."

"I am afraid you are mistaken, Signor Gianelli," interrupted a young man of distinguished appearance, somewhat excitedly. "If Rinaldo himself demanded the postponement, there is sure to be some cause for it."

"Excuse me, Marchese, it is not so," replied the former. "I, as conductor of the grand opera, know best what endless trouble, and what immense sacrifice of time and money it has cost to meet Rinaldo's wishes. He brought the whole theatrical world into confusion with his conditions and requirements, as he demanded changes in the company such as had never been made before, and everything in the same way. As usual, all was acceded to, and all expected at last to be sure of his approval; but now, on arriving from M----, he finds nothing but what is far beneath his anticipations, he orders alterations and dictates improvements in the most inconsiderate manner. In vain was it attempted to dissuade him, through Signora Biancona; he threatened to withdraw the entire opera, and--" here the maestro shrugged his shoulders satirically, "his Excellency the Director would not take the responsibility of such a misfortune upon his shoulders. He promised everything, conceded everything, and as it was quite impossible to carry out the so peremptorily demanded additions in such a short time, even although ordered by the sovereign Signor Rinaldo, the performance was obliged to be postponed until the next season."

"The Director in this case was quite right to give way to the wish, or, if you like it, whim of the composer," said the young Marchese decidedly. "The company would never have forgiven it if bad management had robbed them of one of Rinaldo's operas. It is known that he would be capable of carrying out his threat, and really withdrawing his work, and with such an alternative before him, nothing remained but to give way unconditionally."

"Certainly; my objection only concerns this species of terrorism which a strange composer allows himself here, in the heart of Italy, inasmuch as he compelled the inhabitants to content themselves with his essentially German ideas of music."

"Especially when these same inhabitants have twice made a *fiasco* of an opera, while every new creation of Rinaldo's is greeted with tempestuous applause by the audience," whispered the Marchese to his neighbour.

The latter, an Englishman, looked much bored. He only understood Italian imperfectly, and the rapid, vivacious conversation was therefore greatly lost to him. Nevertheless he answered the Marchese's low spoken and contemptuous remark with a solemn nod, and then looked attentively at the maestro, as if the latter had become an object of curiosity for him.

"We are speaking of Rinaldo's new opera," said the officer, turning and explaining politely to the stranger, who so far had remained a silent listener, and now replied in foreign sounding, but yet fluent Italian--"I just heard the name. No doubt some musical celebrity."

The gentlemen looked in speechless astonishment at the inquirer; only the maestro's face betrayed unmistakable satisfaction that there was at least one person in the world who did not know this name.

"Some celebrity!" repeated Marchese Tortoni. "Excuse me Signor Capitano, but you must have been a long time at sea, and perhaps come from another hemisphere?"

"Direct from the South Sea Islands!" said the Captain with a pleasant smile, notwithstanding the ironical tone of the question, "and as there, unfortunately, they are not so well acquainted with the artistic productions of the present times as might be desired in the interests of civilisation, I beg to receive assistance in my deplorable ignorance."

"We are speaking about the greatest and most charming of our present composers," said the Marchese. "He is certainly by birth a German, but since some years has belonged to us exclusively. He lives and works only on Italian ground, and we are proud to be permitted to call him ours. It will be easy for you to make his personal acquaintance this evening. He is sure to appear!"

"With Signora Biancona--of course!" interrupted the officer, "have you had an opportunity already of hearing our beautiful *prima donna*?"

The Captain made a gesture of denial. "I only arrived a few days since; however, I saw her some years previously in my home, where she gained her first laurels."

"Ah, she was a rising star then," cried the others. "To be sure she laid the foundation of her fame in the north. She returned to us as a known actress.

But now she stands undoubtedly at the height of her power. You must hear her, and hear her in one of Rinaldo's operas, when you can admire her in all her glory."

"To be sure, as then one fire ignites the other," added the young Marchese. "At any rate you will find in the Signora of to-day a brilliantly beautiful apparition. Do not delay an introduction and interview with her."

"Provided it be agreeable to Signor Rinaldo," said the maestro, joining in again. "Otherwise you may attempt to approach her in vain."

"Has Rinaldo power to decide such points?" asked the Captain lightly.

"Well, at least he takes the right to do so. He is so used to being master and ruler everywhere that he tries it here also, and, alas, not without result. I do not understand Biancona. An actress of her importance, a woman of her beauty, to allow herself to be so completely ruled by a man."

"But he is Rinaldo," laughed the officer, "and that is saying enough. Let us confess it, Tortoni, we can none of us compete with his successes. All hearts fly towards him, wherever he appears; so at last it is no wonder if even a Biancona bows willingly before the magic which this man seems to bear about him."

"Hum, it is not done quite so willingly," said Gianelli, grimly. "Signora is passionate in the highest degree, but Rinaldo, if possible, even surpasses her. Between them it is quite as often storm as sunshine, and furious scenes are the order of the day."

"This Rinaldo appears to govern all society as well as his audiences," said the Captain, now turning exclusively to the conductor. "Do people submit to such a thing from one single man, and he a stranger?"

"Because all are blind, and will be to every other merit," cried the maestro with suppressed violence. "When society once raises an idol to a throne, it carries on its adoration until it becomes ridiculous. They regularly worship Rinaldo, so it is no wonder if his pride and self-appreciation become boundless, and he thinks he can trample on all with impunity who do not pay him homage."

The Captain looked steadily and with a peculiar smile at the excited Italian.

"It is a pity that such talent should have so dark a side! But after all, it is not so much talent as fashion, whim of the public, unmerited success; do not you think so?"

Gianelli would probably have agreed with all his heart, but the other gentlemen's presence put some restraint upon him.

"The public generally decides in such cases," he replied, prudently, "and here it is extravagant in its favours. For my part, I maintain, without wishing in the least to detract from Rinaldo's fame, that he might compose the most meritless work and they would extol it to the skies, because it came from him."

"Very probably," agreed the stranger. "And possibly this new opera is meritless. I am certainly of your opinion, and shall assuredly--"

"I advise you, Signor to withhold your opinion until you have become acquainted with Rinaldo's works," interrupted the Marchese, sharply. "He has certainly made the unpardonable mistake of attaining the summit of fame in one unbroken course of triumph, and of acquiring greatness to which no other can reach so easily. This cannot be forgiven him in certain circles, and he must do penance for it on every occasion. Follow my advice."

The Captain bowed slightly. "With pleasure, and all the more as it is my brother whom you have defended so eloquently, Marchese."

This explanation, made with a most pleasant smile, naturally created a great sensation in the group. Marchese Tortoni took a step backwards in astonishment, and examined the speaker from head to foot. The maestro became pale and bit his lips, while the officer with difficulty refrained from laughing. The Englishman this time understood enough of the conversation to comprehend the trick which had been played, and which seemed to arouse his entire satisfaction. He smiled with an expression of extreme contentment, and with long strides crossed over immediately to the Captain, at whose side he placed himself silently, thus giving him an unmistakable sign of approval.

"The musical name of my brother appears only to be known to these gentlemen," continued Hugo unabashed, "mine doubtless sounded too foreign to you in the general introduction. We have, indeed, no reason to deny our relationship."

"Ah, Signor Capitano, I had heard already of your intended arrival," cried the Marchese, offering his hand with evident heartiness, "but it was not fair to cheat us with an *incognito*. To one, at least, it has caused bitter confusion, although he richly deserved the lesson."

Hugo looked round at once for the maestro, who had preferred to retire unnoticed. "I wished to reconnoitre the ground a little," retorted he, laughing, "and that was only possible so long as my *incognito* lasted. But it would soon have reached its termination, as I expect Reinhold every moment; he was detained in the town, while I drove on in advance. Ah, he is there already."

"I? Oh, I mean nothing, excepting, perhaps, that it must be an elevating sensation to have thus the entire fate of a man--or even a family--in one's hands; in tearing him away from his 'fetters,' one must feel in such a case something like an earthly providence. Is it not so, Signora?"

Beatrice had started slightly at these words, whether from astonishment or anger was not easy to decide. Her eyes met his; but this time they measured one another, as two antagonists do. The Italian's glance flashed; but the Captain bore it so firmly and quietly, that she felt it was not such an easy game opposite those clear brown eyes, which dared fearlessly to break a lance with her.

"I believe Rinaldo has every cause to be grateful to this providence," replied she, proudly. "Perhaps he would have sunk amid circumstances and surroundings which were unworthy of him, if it had not aroused his genius and shown him the path to greatness."

"Perhaps," said Hugo, coolly. "But people maintain that real genius never does sink, and the more difficulties it has to penetrate the more do they strengthen its power; however, that, of course, is also one of the northern pedantic views. The result has decided in favour of your view, Signora, and success is a god to which all bow."

He inclined his head and retired. He had said all this in the lightest conversational tone, apparently quite unmeaningly, but Signora Biancona must surely have felt the bitterness which lay in the Captain's words, for she pressed her lips together in most intense internal irritation, and her fan was moved almost furiously.

He really appeared at that moment on the terrace, and the maestro would have had fresh opportunity to give vent to his anger at the "adoration, which became ridiculous," as the sudden cessation of all conversation, the interest with which all eyes were directed to one point, the movement which spread through all the company, was only due to Reinhold's entrance.

Reinhold himself had become quite different in these years--quite different. The young genius who had once fought so impatiently against the confining limits and prejudices of his surroundings, had raised himself to be a renowned composer, whose name extended beyond the boundaries of Italy and his home, whose works were familiar on the stages of all capitals; to whom fame and honour, money and triumph, flowed in richest abundance. The same mighty change had also been carried out in his exterior, and this alteration was not at all disadvantageous, as instead of the pale, serious youth, there now stood a man in whom it was evident that he was at home with life and the world, and only in the man did the always peculiarly attractive style of his beauty manifest itself entirely. The proud self-consciousness which now rested upon his *spirituel* brow, and showed itself in all his features and his whole bearing, became them well, but there lay also a heavy shadow on this brow and on those features which happiness had surely never placed there. His mouth curved with harsh mockery, with contemptuous bitterness, and the former spark slumbered no more in the depths of his eyes; now a flame shone there, burning, destroying, flashing almost demonlike at every emotion. Whatever this face might have gained outwardly, *peace* spoke no more from within.

He conducted Signora Biancona on his arm, no longer the youthful *prima donna* of a second-rate Italian opera company, which gave wandering performances in the north, but a star of European renown, who, after having gathered laurels and triumphs in all important places, now occupied the first position at the theatre of her native town. Marchese Tortoni was right; she was dazzlingly beautiful, this woman; there was the old burning glance, which once understood how to set on fire the honourable patrician blood of the noble Hanseatic town, only now it appeared to have become more glowing, more scorching; there was still the countenance, with its witch-like entrancing magic, the figure with its noble plastic limbs, only everything seemed fuller, more voluptuous. The flower had developed to the ripest, almost over-ripe splendour; she still bloomed, her beauty was still at its zenith, if even one could not but acknowledge that perhaps in the course of the next few years the limits would be already passed beyond which she would be tending irrecoverably to her descent.

Both, especially Reinhold, were seized upon the moment they arrived. All crowded around him; all sought his vicinity, his conversation. In a few moments he had become the centre of the assemblage, and some time elapsed before he could withdraw from all the attentions and flatteries in order to look round for his brother, who had stood somewhat aloof.

"There you are at last, Hugo," said he, approaching, "I missed you already. You make one seek you?"

"It was not possible to break through that triple circle of admirers, which surrounds you like a Chinese wall; I have not attempted such a piece of daring, but indulged in contemplating what happiness it is to possess a celebrated brother."

"Yes, this everlasting crush is really oppressive," said Reinhold, with an expression which showed not contented triumph, but, on the contrary, unmistakable weariness; "however come now, I will introduce you to Beatrice."

"Beatrice?--Ah, Signora Vampire! *must* I, Reinhold?"

His brother's look became overcast. "Certainly you must. You cannot avoid seeing her in my company, much and often. She is beautiful, and with reason wonders it has not already been done. What is it, Hugo? You appear wishful to evade this introduction altogether, and yet you do not know Beatrice even."

"I do, though," replied the Captain shortly. "I have seen her already at a concert on the stage at H----."

"But never spoken to her. It is odd one must almost compel you to do what any other would look upon as a privilege! Usually you are the first, when acquaintance with a beautiful woman is in question."

Hugo replied nothing, but followed without farther protest. Signora Biancona, as was her custom, was surrounded by a circle of gentlemen, and engaged in most lively conversation, which she, however, broke off immediately the two appeared. Reinhold presented his brother to her. Beatrice turned to the latter with all her fascinations.

"Do you know, Captain, I have been angry with you already, without knowing you?" she began. "Reinhold was beside himself when he received the news of your arrival. He left me in M---- in the most ungallant manner, in order to hasten towards you. I had to undertake my return journey alone."

Hugo bowed politely, but more distantly than was his wont to a lady, nor did he appear to notice that Beatrice's beautiful hand was extended confidently to Rinaldo's brother, at least he utterly resisted the temptation of kissing it, which was certainly expected.

"I am very unhappy, Signora, at having roused your ill-will. But o who disposes so exclusively of Reinhold's presence and company, should possess liberality enough to forego it a short time in favour of his brother."

He looked round for Reinhold, but the latter was already engaged.

"I resign myself," said Beatrice, still with charming friendliness, "or rather I must still resign myself, as, since you came, I have seen little enough of Rinaldo. There will remain no other remedy than to beg you to accompany him when he comes to see me."

Hugo made a somewhat measured gesture of thanks--

"You are very kind, Signora. I shall seize with pleasure the opportunity of becoming better acquainted with my brother's admired--Muse."

Signora Biancona, smiled--

"Has he called me so to you? To be sure the name is not strange in our circle of friends. Rinaldo gave it me once, when I led his first steps to the path of art. A somewhat romantic designation, especially according to German views, is it not, Signor? You hardly have such in your north?"

"Sometimes," said the Captain quietly, "only with a slight difference. With us, muses are ideal, floating in unattainable heights. Here they are--beautiful women. An undeniable advantage for the artist!"

The words sounded like a compliment, and adhered steadily to the playful tone which Beatrice herself had commenced; nevertheless she cast a quick searching glance at the speaker's face--perhaps she saw the sparkling scorn in it--as she answered sharply--

"For my part, I confess to have no sympathy with the north. Simply because compelled, did I pass some short time there, and could only breathe again when Italy's sky rose above me. We southerners cannot succeed in submitting to the icy, pedantic rules which confine society there, to the fetters which they would wish even to impose upon artists."

Hugo leant with perfect indifference against the marble balustrade.

"Good God, that is of no importance. They are easily broken, and then one is free as the birds in the air. Reinhold proved that sufficiently, and now he has foresworn home and pedantic rules for ever, which is entirely due to you, Signora."

Beatrice used her fan violently, although at this moment the evening breeze blew refreshingly cool.

"How do you mean, Signor?" asked she, quickly.

CHAPTER VIII

Meanwhile Hugo had sought his brother, whom he found in conversation with Marchese Tortoni; both stood a little apart from the rest of the company.

"No, no, Cesario," said Reinhold, at that moment, refusing something. "I have only shortly returned from M----, and cannot possibly think of leaving town again. Perhaps later--"

"But the opera is postponed," interrupted the young Marchese, in a beseeching tone, "and the heat begins to be oppressive. You are sure to select some *villegiatura* in a few weeks. Come to my assistance, Captain," said he, turning to Hugo, just then approaching. "You intend, surely, to become acquainted with our south, and there is no better opportunity than in my Mirando."

"Do you know the Marchese already?" asked Reinhold. "Then I need not introduce you."

"Certainly not," replied Hugo, mischievously. "I introduced myself personally to these gentlemen, just as they were sitting in judgment upon you, and I had the harmless pleasure, as an unknown listener, of rousing them against you by casual remarks. Unfortunately it only succeeded with one. Marchese Tortoni, on the contrary, took your part most passionately; I had to feel the whole weight of his displeasure, as I allowed myself to doubt your talent."

Reinhold shook his head. "Has he been playing his tricks already, Cesario? Take care, Hugo, with your jokes! We are here on Italian ground, where people do not take such things so lightly as in our home."

"Well, in this case the name was only required to reconcile us," said the Marchese, smiling. "But we are losing the thread of our discussion entirely," continued he, impatiently. "I have still received no reply to my request. I count positively upon your visit, Rinaldo; naturally on yours also, Signor."

"I am my brother's guest," exclaimed Hugo, to whom the last words were addressed. "Such a decision depends upon him and--Signora Biancona."

"Upon Beatrice! How so?" asked Reinhold, quickly.

"Well, she is already greatly annoyed that my presence keeps you so much from her. It is decidedly a question whether she will set you at liberty for any time, as Marchese Tortoni seems to wish."

"Do you think I should allow myself to be so entirely governed by her whims?" Reinhold's voice betrayed rising irritation. "I shall have to show that I can form a decision without her leave. We will come, Cesario, next month, I promise you."

An expression of great pleasure passed over the young man's face at this rapid, impetuous assent; he turned politely to the Captain.

"Rinaldo knows my Mirando well, and has always praised it. I hope also to be able to make your stay agreeable to you. The villa is beautifully situated, close to the sea shore--"

"And isolated," said Reinhold, with a peculiar mixture of melancholy and longing. "One can breathe there while one is almost suffocated in the drawing-room atmosphere. But our friends are going to dinner," said he, turning the conversation, with an upward glance to the terrace. "We must, I suppose, join the others. Will you take Beatrice to dinner, Hugo?"

"No, thank you," declined the Captain, coolly. "That is surely your exclusive right. I do not wish to dispute it."

"Your conversation with her was remarkably short," said Reinhold, as together they ascended the steps of the terrace. "What was the matter with you both?"

"Nothing particular. A little outpost skirmish; nothing more. Signora and I have taken up our positions towards one another at once. I hope you do not object."

He received no answer, as Signora Biancona's silk dress rustled close by them, and the next moment stood between the brothers. The Captain bowed low, with consummate gallantry, before the beautiful woman. It would indeed have been impossible to find the least fault with this mode of greeting, and Beatrice acknowledged it with an inclination of her head, but the glance which she shot towards him showed sufficiently that she also had taken up her position. The intense hatred of the roused southerner blazed in her eye, only for a moment to be sure; the next she turned round, laid her hand on Reinhold's arm, to let him lead her into the dining-room.

"That seems to me neither more nor less than a declaration of war," murmured Hugo, as he followed the pair. "Wordless, but sufficiently comprehensible. The enmity has begun--at your commands, Signora."

Marchese Tortoni was not wrong in his remarks; the heat, notwithstanding the early season of the year, began to be oppressive. The season was not over yet, but many families had already exchanged their residence in the town for the usual *villegiatura* in the mountains or by the seaside, and the rest of the society was also on the point of dispersing itself earlier than usual to all points of the compass, until autumn brought them together once more.

In Signora Biancona's house no preparations had been made so far which might lead to the inference of a speedy departure, and yet one seemed to be under discussion in the interview which had just taken place between her and Reinhold Almbach. The two were alone in the singer's brilliantly and dazzlingly illuminated saloon; but Beatrice's beautiful face bore an expression of unmistakable excitement. Leaning against the cushions of the divan, her lips pressed angrily together, she plucked to pieces one of the beautiful bouquets which ornamented the celebrated actress' reception-room so plentifully; while Reinhold was walking up and down the room with folded arms and gloomily clouded brow. It only required a single glance to guess that one of those stormy scenes was being enacted which Maestro Gianelli declared were as frequent between the two as was sunshine.

"I beg you, Beatrice, spare me any more of these exhibitions," said Reinhold, with great violence. "You cannot alter an affair already determined upon. Marchese Tortoni received my promise, and our departure for Mirando is arranged for to-morrow."

"Well, then, you must retract this promise," replied Beatrice, in the same tone. "You gave it without my knowledge, gave it weeks ago, and then we had already decided to spend our *villegiatura* in the mountains this year."

"Certainly! And I shall follow you there as soon as I return from Mirando."

"As soon as you return! As if Tortoni would not try every means to chain you there as usual, and if now, in addition, you go in your brother's company, it is a matter of course that you will be kept away from me as long as possible."

Reinhold stopped suddenly, and a dark look was turned towards her.

"Will you not have the goodness to leave this wearisome, exhausted subject at last?" asked he, sharply. "I know already quite well enough that there is no sympathy between you and Hugo; but he, at any rate, spares me any dissertations upon it, and does not require me to share his sympathies and antipathies. Besides, you must allow that he has never been impolite towards you."

Beatrice threw her bouquet aside and rose. "Oh, yes, I allow that, certainly; and it is just this courteousness which annoys me so much. The agreeable conversations, with the everlasting, scornful smile on his lips; the attentions, with contempt in his eyes; that is quite the German manner, from which I suffered so much in your north, which governs and rules us in the so-called circles of society, which knows how to restrain us there, even when fighting ever so bitterly with any one. Your brother understands that perfectly; nothing hits him, nothing wounds him; everything glances off from his everlasting, mocking smile. I--I hate him, and he me not less."

"With difficulty," said Reinhold bitterly, "as you are such a mistress of the art, as few others can be. I have often enough seen that, when you have imagined yourself insulted by anyone. With you it overflows all bounds at once. But this time, you will remember, that it is my brother against whom this hatred is directed, and that through it I am not disposed to let myself be robbed of our first short meeting for years. I shall endure no insult, no attack, upon Hugo."

"Because you love him more than me," cried Beatrice, wildly. "Because I count for nothing beside your brother. To be sure, what am I to you?"

And now the way was opened to a regular flood of reproaches, complaints, and threats, which finally ended in a torrent of tears. All the passion of the Italian broke forth; but Reinhold seemed to be moved to nothing less than concession by it. He attempted to restrain her several times, and as he did not succeed, he stamped furiously with his foot.

"Once more, Beatrice, cease these scenes. You know that you never gain anything with me by them, and I should have thought you had already found by experience that I am not such a slave without a will, that a word or a caprice from you is a command. I shall not put up with these continual exhibitions any longer, which you call forth on every occasion."

He went furiously to the balcony, and, turning his back upon the room, looked down into the street, where the busy movement of the Corso was visible. For a few minutes Beatrice's passionate sobs were heard in the saloon; then all was still, and immediately after she placed a hand on his shoulder, as he stood at the window.

"Rinaldo!"

Half-reluctantly he turned round. His glance met Beatrice's glowing dark eye; a tear still stood in it, but it was no longer a tear of anger, and her voice, just now so excited, had a soft, melting ring in it.

"You say I am a mistress in the art of hating. Only in hating, Rinaldo? You have often enough experienced the contrary."

Reinhold now turned completely to her, and returned from the balcony.

"I know that you can love," replied he, more mildly, "love warmly and wholly. But you can also torment with this love; that I have to feel every day."

"And you would wish to flee this torment, at least for a time?"

A deep reproach sounded in her voice. Almbach made an impatient movement.

"I seek peace, Beatrice," said he, "and that I do not find at all near you. You can only breathe in constant heat and excitement, both are your conditions of life, and you drag your entire surroundings with you in the everlasting fire of your nature. I--am tired."

"Of society or of me?" asked Beatrice, with freshly rising fury.

"Can you not cease from seeking a stab in every word?" asked Reinhold, angrily. "I see we do not understand each other again to-day. Adieu!"

"You are going!" cried the Italian, half-frightened, half-threateningly. "And with this farewell for a separation of weeks!"

Reinhold, who was already at the door, thought a moment and turned slowly round.

"Ah, yes; I forgot the departure. Farewell, Beatrice!"

But he was not permitted to make his farewell so easily. Signora Biancona had long since learned not to defy for any time the man who now understood how to bend her otherwise capricious will to his own, and when he again drew near to her all farther opposition was at an end. Her voice trembled as she asked softly, "And you will really go alone, without me?"

"Beatrice--"

"Alone, without me?" repeated she, more passionately. Reinhold made an attempt to withdraw his hand from her, but it remained only an attempt.

"Cesario expects me positively," he said, deprecatingly, "and I have already explained that you cannot accompany me--"

"Not to Mirando," interrupted Beatrice, "I know that. But what prevents my altering the original plan, and making my first summer stay in S---- instead of in the mountains, the great resort of all strangers? It is near enough to Mirando, half-an-hour by boat would bring you across to me. If I were to follow you--may I, Rinaldo?"

This tone of flattering entreaty was irresistible, and her glance begged still more. Reinhold looked down silently at the beautiful woman, the possession of whose love once appeared to him the highest prize of happiness. The magic still exercised its old power, and exercised it now most strongly when he was attempting to escape from it. The concession was not made in words, but Beatrice saw, as he bent towards her, that she had conquered this time. When he really left her, half-an-hour later, the change in the plan of her journey was quite decided upon, and their farewell was not for a separation of weeks, but only of days.

It was already becoming dark, and the moon was rising slowly, when Reinhold reached his own abode, which lay at some distance, in a more open part of the town. On entering his reception-room he found the Captain there, who appeared just to have been giving his servant an impressive lecture, as Jonas stood before him with a most rueful countenance, which was comically mixed with suppressed indignation, to find words for which his master's presence only prevented him.

"What is it?" asked Reinhold, somewhat astonished.

"An inquisitorial enquiry," replied Hugo, annoyed. "For years I have taken trouble in vain with this obstinate sinner and incorrigible woman-hater, but neither teaching nor example--Jonas, you are to go instantly up to the Padrona, beg her pardon, and promise to be more mannerly in future. March! go along!"

"I shall be obliged to send him back to the 'Ellida' at last," continued he, turning to his brother, when Jonas had left the room. "The ship's cat is the only female person there which he has near him; and it is to be hoped he will not quarrel with it."

Reinhold threw himself on a seat. "I wish I had your unconquerable humour, your happy gift of taking life like a game. I never could do it."

"No, the ground notes of your being were always elegiac," said the Captain. "I believe you never looked upon me as quite equal to yourself in birth, as I could not take such ideal romantic flight to the heights, nor penetrate to the depths, like your artistic natures. We sailors are happy on the surface, and if now and then a storm should disturb the deep, it does not matter to us, we remain above."

"Quite true," said Reinhold, gloomily. "May you always, stay on your sunny, bright surface! Believe me, Hugo, it is only muddy below in the depths, where people seek for treasures; and an icy breath blows above in the height, where one dreamed of nothing but sunlight. I have tasted both."

Hugo looked searchingly at his brother, who lay more than sat on his seat, his head leaning back, as if tired to death, while his gloomy eyes wandered out over the gardens of the neighbourhood, and at last remained fixed on the faintly illumined horizon, where the last rays of daylight just disappeared.

"Listen, Reinhold; you do not please me at all," he broke forth suddenly. "After years I come to see my brother again, whose name fills the whole world, to whom fate has given everything it can give to one man. I find you at the height of renown and success--and I expected to find you different."

"And how, then?" asked Reinhold, without raising his head or turning his eyes from the darkening evening sky.

"I do not know," said the Captain, earnestly. "But I know that after a fortnight only I cannot endure this life, which you have led for years. This restless rushing from pleasure to pleasure, without any satisfaction; this constant wavering between wild excitement and deadly exhaustion does not suit my nature. You should put a bridle on yours."

Reinhold made a half-impatient movement. "Folly. I have become accustomed to it for long; and besides, you do not understand it, Hugo."

"Possibly. At any rate I do not require to deaden my feelings."

Reinhold started up. A glance of burning anger met his brother, who attempted to pierce so far into his innermost thoughts, and who continued, quite unmoved--

"It is only a means of deadening your feelings which you struggle for day after day, which you seek everywhere without finding. Give up this life, I entreat you. You will ruin yourself, body and mind, by it; you must succumb to it at last."

"How long is it since the joyous Captain of the 'Ellida' has become a preacher of moralities," scoffed Reinhold, with as much scornful expression as he could use. "Who would have thought long ago that you would lecture me in this manner. But do not take any trouble about my conversion, Hugo. I have foresworn all the pious ideas of my youth, once for all."

The Captain was silent. This was again the tone of wounding scorn with which Reinhold made himself unapproachable the moment such topics were touched upon; this tone, which made all influence impossible, which jarred so upon every recollection of youth, and made the formerly warm bond between the brothers strange and cold. Hugo did not even try to-day to alter it; he knew that it would be in vain. Turning away, he took up a book which was lying on the table, and began turning over its leaves.

"I have never heard a single word from you about my compositions," began Reinhold, again, after a momentary silence. "You have had an opportunity here of becoming acquainted with my operas. How do you like them?"

"I am no connoisseur of music," said Hugo, evasively.

"I know that, and therefore I lay some value on your opinion, because it is that of the unprejudiced, but acute public. How do you like my music?"

The Captain threw the book on the table.

"It is agreeable and--" he stopped.

"And?"

"Unbridled as yourself. You and your tones go beyond all bounds."

"An annihilating criticism," said Reinhold, half-struck by it. "It is well that I should hear it; you would fare badly in the circle of my admirers. How then do you allow that there is anything agreeable in it?"

"When you, yourself speak--yes!" explained Hugo, decidedly, "but that is seldom enough. Generally this strange element predominates which has given the turn to your talent, and still rules it. I cannot help it, Reinhold, but this influence which from the commencement you have followed, which all the world prizes as so elevating, has brought no good, not even to the artist. Without it you might not have been so celebrated, but undoubtedly greater."

"Truly, Beatrice is right, when she dreads you as her implacable opponent," remarked Reinhold, with undisguised bitterness. "Certainly, she only thinks of a personal prejudice. That you do not even allow the value of her artistic influence upon me would indeed be new to her."

Hugo shrugged his shoulders. "She has quite drawn you into the Italian style. You always storm when others only play, but it is all the same. Why do you not write German music? But what am I talking about? You have turned your back upon home and all its belongings for ever."

Reinhold rested his head on his hand. "Yes certainly--for ever."

"That almost sounds like regret," hazarded the Captain, looking with fixed scrutiny at his brother's face. The latter looked up darkly.

"What do you mean? Do you perhaps think I regret the old chains, because I have not found the happiness dreamed of in freedom? If I tried any communication it would--"

"Ah, you did attempt some communication with your wife?"

"With Ella?" asked Reinhold, and there was again the old mixture of pity and contempt, which betrayed itself in his voice the moment he spoke of his wife. "What good could that have done? You know how I left; it was done by a complete rupture with her parents, and therefore naturally a narrow, dependent nature like Ella's would join in the verdict of condemnation if it were ever even able to raise itself to a verdict of its own. If the breach between us was formerly wide, now, after all that has happened, it has become impassable. No, there could be no talk of that, but I wished to receive news of my child. I could not bear longer to have my boy so far away, not to be able to see him, not even to possess a picture of him. I wanted his at any price, therefore I chose the shortest means, and wrote to the mother."

"Well, and--?" asked Hugo, with interest.

Reinhold laughed bitterly--

"T might have spared myself the humiliation. No answer came--that certainly was answer enough, but I wanted just to know how the child was; I thought of the possibility of a mistake, of its being lost--what does one not think of in such a case?--and wrote again. The letter came back unopened"--he clenched his fist in wild anger--"unopened, to me! It is my uncle's work; there is no doubt of it. Ella would never have dared to offer it to me."

"Do you think so? You do not know your wife. She certainly has 'dared' to offer it, and she alone could dare it, as her parents have been dead some years."

Reinhold turned round quickly--

"How do you know that? Are you still in communication with H----?"

"No," said the Captain, quietly; "you may imagine that the state of mind which existed in the family towards you was also partly carried over to me. Since I left H---- at that time, a few days after you did, I have never revisited it, but I correspond still with the former bookkeeper of the firm of Almbach, who has taken over the business, and continues it on his own account. I heard a few things from him."

"And you only tell me this now, after being together for nearly a fortnight?" cried Reinhold, almost furiously.

"I have naturally not wished to touch upon a subject which it seemed to me you wished to avoid," answered Hugo coolly.

Reinhold walked up and down the room a few times--

"Her parents are dead, then? And Ella and the child?"

"You need not be anxious about them; my uncle left a good fortune, much more than people thought."

"I knew he was richer than he wished to be deemed," said Reinhold quickly, "and this certainly alone gave me perfect freedom of action in my departure. I was not necessary for my wife and child. They were safe from any change of fate, without even my presence. But where are they now? Still in H----?"

"Herr Consul Erlau was appointed the boy's guardian," informed Hugo, rather shortly and distantly. "He appears also to have taken very active interest in the deserted wife, as directly after expiration of the time of mourning she moved into his house with the child. There both were still living, half-a-year ago; so far my news extends."

"Indeed?" said Reinhold thoughtfully, "only I do not understand how Ella, with her education and her habits, can possibly exist in the splendid establishment of the Erlaus. I suppose she will have arranged a few back rooms so as never to appear, or, notwithstanding her fortune, have undertaken the post of housekeeper. She will never be able to rise above this ambition. Had it not been so, I should have borne much, indeed all--for the child's sake."

He went to the window, pushed it open, and leant out. The evening air blew cool into the close room, where now a long silence ensued, as even the Captain seemed to have no more inclination to prolong the conversation. After a time he arose.

"Our departure in the morning is arranged rather early; we must be awake betimes. Good night, Reinhold!"

"Good night!" replied Reinhold, without turning round.

Hugo left the room. "I wish this Circe of a Beatrice could see him at such moments," muttered he, shutting the door. "You have conquered, Signora, and torn him to yourself as your indisputable property--you have not made him happy."

Reinhold remained a few moments longer immovable, at his place; then he raised himself and went over to his work room. He had to pass through several apartments in order to reach it. This abode, which occupied the entire ground floor of the roomy villa, was not so brilliant as that of Signora Biancona, but yet more extravagantly furnished, as the magnificence which reigned there was here ten times surpassed by the artistic decorations of the rooms; so there pictures hung on the walls, statues stood in the window niches, whose value could only be estimated by thousands; here were produced masterly copies of the most splendid art treasures of Italy. Wherever the eye turned, it met vases, busts, drawings and beautiful works, which elsewhere would have been each alone the ornament of any drawing-room, and which here, scattered everywhere, only served as additional decorations. Everywhere was wealth of beauty and art such as only a Rinaldo could gather around him in so lavish a manner, to whom gold as well as fame flowed in never-ceasing plenty, and who was accustomed to throw the former away quite recklessly.

In the middle of the study there stood a splendid piano, the gift of an enthusiastic circle of admirers, who wished to offer a visible testimony of their thanks to the master; the writing-table was covered with cards and letters, which bore the names of the first people in the kingdom, both as regards birth and genius, and which here were indifferently thrust aside, without the recipient placing the least value on them; from the principal wall, a life-sized picture of Beatrice Biancona looked down, painted by a celebrated hand, most charmingly represented, a really speaking likeness. She wore the fanciful costume of one of her chief parts in an opera of Rinaldo's, through the successful representation of whose works she herself had only risen to be an actress of the first order. The painter had succeeded in embodying the utterly infatuating magic, the glowing charm of the original, in this portrait. The beautiful figure appeared half-turned to the piano in an inimitably graceful pose, and the dark eyes gazed with deceptively life-like truth down upon the man whom they had kept so long already in indissoluble bonds, as if even here, in the sacred place of his works and labour, they would not leave him alone.

CHAPTER IX

Reinhold sat at his piano, improvising. The room was not lighted, only the moon's rays, streaming fully in, hung over the flood of tones, which now rose as if the storm were raging in its waves, now rolling up mountains high, and then again disclosing the depths of an abyss. The melodies flowed forth passionately, glowing, intoxicatingly, and then suddenly they would start and change as if to harsh dissonance, to jarring discord. Those were the tones with which Rinaldo for years had reigned in the realms of music, with which he carried the crowd away to admiration; perhaps because they lent language to that demon-like element which slumbers in every one's breast, and of which every one is conscious, partly with dread, partly with secret shuddering. There lay, too, in these melodies something of that wild rush from pleasure to pleasure, of that rapid change from feverish excitement to deadly exhaustion, from that striving to benumb all feeling, which, sought for ever, is never found; and yet there rang forth something powerful, eternal, which had nothing in common with that element with which it fought, and which was raised above it, only to be wrecked within it at last.

The perfume of oranges rose from the gardens and streamed in through the widely-opened doors on to the balcony, and was wafted intoxicatingly through the apartments. Clear, full of great beauty and intense peace, lay the moonlight above the old town, and the dim distance disappeared in the blue, misty vapour. The fountain rustled dreamily amongst the blooming trees, and the light which shone in the falling drops illuminated with powerful distinctness the whole row of apartments, with their marble treasures of art; it illuminated the picture in the richly gilt frame, so that the witch-like, beautiful figure above seemed to live; and the same light fell upon the countenance of the man, whose brow, amid all this beauty and all this peace, remained so heavily overcast.

How many years, and, indeed, much besides which weighed more heavily than years only, lay between those long northern winter nights on which the young musician created his first compositions, and this balmy moonlight night of the south, on which the world-renowned Rinaldo repeated, in endless variations, the principal theme of his newest opera. And yet all vanished in this hour. Softly, recollection passed before him, and let long-forgotten days live again, long-forgotten pictures stand before him; the little garden house, with its old-fashioned furniture, and the stunted vines over the window, the miserable little strip of garden with its few trees and shrubs, and the high, prison-like walls around it; the narrow, gloomy house, with the so intensely hated business-room. Faint, colourless pictures--and yet they would not give way, as above them floated smilingly a pair of large, deep, blue child's eyes, which only there had shone for the father, and which here, in this orbit, full of poetry and beauty, he sought for in vain. He had seen them so often in his child's face, and also once somewhere else. The remembrance of this was certainly but dim, almost forgotten; they had only then shown themselves to him for a moment, before being veiled again immediately, as they had been for years; but it was still those eyes, which hovered before him, as now, out of the storming and rolling tones, a magically sweet melody arose. An endless longing spoke in it, a pain which his lips would not utter, and thus formed a bridge across into the far distant past. Now had genius burst the fetters which then oppressed and confined him; now he stood aloft on the once dreamed-of heights. All that life and success, fame and love could give had become his portion, and now--again like a storm, it swept over the notes, wild, passionate, bacchante-like, and through it ever again that melody came plaintively, with its touching pain, its restless longing, which could not be pacified.

"I fear our captain will not endure Mirando much longer. It is dangerous having the sea thus ever before his eyes; he gazes over it with such longing, as if the sooner that he could sail away from us the better."

With these words Marchese Tortoni turned to his guest, who, for the last quarter of an hour had taken hardly any part in the conversation, and whom the young lord just caught in the act of a surreptitious yawn.

"Indeed not," said Hugo, defending himself. "I only feel myself so utterly unimportant and ignorant in these ideal art discussions, and so deeply impressed with the sense of my ignorance, that I have just gone hurriedly through all the words of command during a storm, in order to obtain for myself the consolatory conviction that I do understand something."

"All evasion!" cried the Marchese. "You miss the female element here, which you adore so much, and now appear unable to forego. Unfortunately, my Mirando cannot offer you that charm, as yet. You know I am not married, and have not been able to resolve upon sacrificing my freedom."

"Not resolve upon sacrificing your freedom," intimated Hugo. "My God, that sounds shocking. If you have not yet ascended the highest ladder of earthly happiness, as books express it--"

"Do not believe him, Cesario," broke in Reinhold. "Notwithstanding all his gallantry and knightliness, at heart he is of an icy nature, which nothing warms too easily. He plays with all--has no feeling for any; the ever-recurring romance, which he even sometimes calls passion, lasts just so long as he is on shore, and disappears with the first fresh breeze which wafts his 'Ellida' away on the sea. Nothing has ever yet stirred his heart."

"Abominable character!" cried Hugo, throwing away his cigar. "I protest against it most solemnly."

"Well you, perhaps, maintain that it is untrue?"

The Captain laughed and turned to Tortoni. "I assure you, Signor Marchese, that I too can be unimpeachably true to my beautiful blue ocean bride"--he pointed towards the sea--"to her I am pledged with heart and hand. She alone understands how to chain and hold me fast again and again, and if she do allow me now and then to look into a pair of beautiful eyes, she never tolerates serious faithlessness."

"Until you look at last into a pair of eyes which teach you that you also are not proof against the universal fate of mortals," said Reinhold, half-jokingly, half with a bitterness which was intelligible only to his brother. "There are such eyes."

"Oh, yes, there are such eyes," repeated Hugo, looking out over the sea with an almost dreamy expression.

"Ah, sir, the tone sounds very suspicious," said the Marchese, teasingly. "Perhaps you have already met with those kind of eyes?"

"I?" The Captain had at once thrown off the momentary seriousness, and was again full of the old mischief. "Folly! I hope to defy long enough yet the 'universal doom of mortals.' Do you hear?"

"What a pity you can find no opportunity here of proving this determination," said Cesario. "The only neighbours whom we have keep themselves so secluded that no attempt ever could be made. The young Signora even--"

"A young Signora? Where?" Hugo jumped up eagerly.

The Marchese pointed to a country house, which, barely a mile distant, lay half-hidden in an olive grove.

"The villa Fiorina yonder has been inhabited for some months. So far as I hear they are also countrymen of yours, Germans, who have settled there for the summer; but they appear to make the most perfect solitude and invisibility their law. No one is received, no one allowed to enter. Visitors from S----, taking advantage of their acquaintance at home, were dismissed, without exception, and, as the family confine their walks chiefly to the park and terrace, it is impossible to approach them."

"And the Signora--is she beautiful?" asked Hugo, with most lively eagerness.

Cesario shrugged his shoulders. "With the best will I cannot tell you. I only saw her once slightly, and at some distance. A slight, youthful figure; a head covered with beautiful golden plaits; unfortunately her face was not turned towards me, and I rode pretty quickly past her."

"Without having seen her face? I admire your stoicism, Marchese, but guarantee myself solemnly against the suspicion of doing likewise. By this evening I will bring you and Reinhold information as to whether the Signora be beautiful or no."

"You may find it difficult," laughed the Marchese. "Do you not hear, all entrance is forbidden?"

"Bah! as if that would prevent me!" cried Hugo, confidently. "The affair only now begins to be interesting. An unapproachable villa, an invisible lady, who is, besides, fair and a German. I will enquire into it, thoroughly examine into it. My duty as a countryman requires it."

"Thank God that you put him upon this scent, Cesario," said Reinhold. "Now let us hope that his ill-concealed yawns will not disturb us any more, when we talk of music. I wished to discuss the parts with you again."

The young Marchese had risen and laid his hand entreatingly on Rinaldo's shoulder.

"Well, and the opera? Do you stand immovably by your ultimatum? I assure you, Rinaldo, it is almost impossible to carry out all these alterations by the autumn; I have convinced myself of it. A new postponement will be required, and the public and company have been waiting for months already."

"They must wait longer." The words sounded haughty, and short in their decision.

"Spoken like a dictator," remarked Hugo. "Are you always so autocratic towards the public? The picture which Maestro Gianelli sketches of you appears to possess some very striking traits of resemblance. I believe it was not really so absolutely necessary to bring the entire opera company, including his Excellency the intendant, into such despair as you have done this time."

Reinhold raised his head with all the pride and indifference of the spoilt, admired artist, who is accustomed to see his will obeyed as if it were law, and to whom opposition is considered equal to an insult.

"I dispose of my work and its performance. Either the opera shall be heard in the form I wish, or not at all. I have left them the choice."

"As if there were any choice!" said Cesario, shrugging his shoulders, as he turned to his servant to give him an order, and left the two brothers alone.

"Unfortunately, there appears to be none in this case," said Hugo, looking after his young host. "And Marchese Tortoni will have you on his conscience also, if you become thoroughly spoiled at last with this senseless worship of you. He does his utmost, like the rest of your adoring circle! They set you up in their midst like a Llama, and group themselves respectfully around you to listen to the remarks of your genius, even if it should please your genius to maltreat your infatuated, surrounders. I am sorry for you, Reinhold. You are driving yourself with certainty to the rock on which already so many valuable powers have been wrecked--self-adoration."

"Hum! in the meanwhile you take care that this should not occur," replied Reinhold, sarcastically. "You appear to like the part of the faithful Eckhard in a remarkable degree, and rehearse it at every opportunity; but it is the most thankless of all. Give it up, Hugo! It does not suit your nature in the least."

The Captain knit his brows, but he remained quite calm at the tone, which might easily have irritated another, threw his fowling-piece over his shoulder, and went out. A few minutes later he found himself by the shore, and only when the fresh sea breeze cooled his head, did the Captain's seriousness leave him; he struck at once into the road to the Villa Fiorina.

To tell the truth, Hugo began to be wearied of Mirando and the prevailing artistic atmosphere which the Marchese's inclination and his brother's presence created there. The paradise-like situation of the property was nothing new to the sailor, who knew so well the beauties of the tropical world, and the solitude to which Reinhold gave himself up with an almost sick longing did not at all suit Hugo's joyous nature. Certainly S----, so much frequented by strangers, lay pretty near, but he could not sail over to it too frequently, and thus indicate to the young host that he missed companionship. Therefore this probably beautiful, and at any rate interesting and mysterious neighbour was very welcome, and Hugo resolved immediately to utilise it.

"Let some one else endure these art lovers and art enthusiasts!" said he, annoyed, as he followed the road by the sea. "Half the day long they sit at the piano, and the rest of the time talk of music. Reinhold always is in extremes. From the midst of the wildest life, out of the most senseless excitement, he rushes head over heels into this romantic solitude, and will hear and know of nothing but his music; I only wonder how long it will last. And this Marchese Tortoni? Young, handsome, rich, of a most noble line; this Cesario does not know what better to do with his life than to bury himself for months in his lonely Mirando, to play the *dilettante* in grand style, and, with his endless worship, turn Reinhold's head still more. I know how to spend my time better than that."

At these last words, spoken with great self-satisfaction, the Captain stopped, as the end of his walk was already, so far, attained. Before him lay the Villa Fiorina, shaded by high fir trees and cypresses, and buried almost in blooming shrubs. The house itself appeared magnificent and roomy, but the chief façade as well as the terrace turned towards the sea, and were so thickly overgrown and surrounded by roses and oleander bushes that even Hugo's hawk's eye was not able to penetrate the balmy fortification. A high wall, covered with creeping plants, enclosed the park-like grounds, which terminated in the olive grove which surrounded the estate. It might formerly have been, judging by the size of the grounds, the property of some great family, then, like so many others, have often changed owners, and now served as temporary residence for rich strangers. At all events, in beauty of situation, it did not yield the palm to Marchese Tortoni's highly prized Mirando.

The Captain had already formed his plan of campaign; he therefore only scanned the country slightly, made a vain attempt to obtain a better view of the terrace from the seaward side, measured the height of the garden walls with his eye, in case of accident, and then went direct to the entrance, where he rang the bell, and demanded to see the owners, without hesitation.

The porter, an old Italian, appeared to have received his instruction for the like cases, as, without even asking the stranger's name, he explained shortly and decidedly that his master and mistress received no visits, and he regretted that the Signor had troubled himself in vain.

Hugo coolly drew out a card. "They will make an exception. It is concerning an affair of importance, which requires a personal interview. I will wait here in the meanwhile, as I am sure to be received."

He sat down quietly on the stone bench, and this immovable confidence impressed the porter so much that he really began to believe in the importance of the pretended mission. He disappeared with the card, while Hugo, quite unconcerned as to the possible consequences, awaited the result of his impudent manœ uvre.

The result was unexpectedly favourable, as in a short time a servant appeared and addressed the stranger, who had introduced himself by a German name, in that language, and begged him to enter. He conducted the Captain into a garden parlour and there left him alone, with the intimation that his master would appear immediately.

"I must be a lucky man," said Hugo, himself somewhat surprised at this unexpected, rapid success. "I wish Reinhold and the Marchese could see me now. Inside the 'unapproachable' villa, expecting the lord and master of the same, and only a few doors apart from the blonde Signora. That is certainly enough for the first five minutes, and what my charming brother could not have attained, although all doors fly open before him. But now I must be charming,--in lies, that is to say--what in the world shall I say to this nobleman, to whom I have had myself announced concerning some important affair, without ever having heard a syllable about him, or he of me? Ah! some one or other, on some of my voyages has given me some commission. In the worst case I can always have mistaken the person; in the meanwhile the acquaintance has been begun, and the rest will follow of itself. I will arrange the improvisation according to the character of the person; at any rate I shall not leave the place without having seen the beautiful Signora."

He sat down and began to examine the room in a perfectly calm state of mind. "My respected countrymen appear to belong to the happy minority, who have at their disposal an income of several ten thousands. The entire villa, with the park, rented for their exclusive use--the arrangements made at great cost; one does not find this comfort in the south--brought their own servants with them; I see no fewer than three faces outside, on which German descent is written. Now the question remains, have we to do with the aristocracy or the exchange? I should prefer the latter; I can then pretend it is about some mercantile affairs, while before some great nobleman, in the nonentity of a citizen, I--how, Herr Consul Erlau!"

With this exclamation, made in boundless astonishment, Hugo started back from the doorway in which the well-known figure of the merchant now appeared. The Consul had certainly aged much in the course of years; the once luxuriant dark hair appeared grey and scant; his features bore an expression of unmistakable suffering, and the friendly good will which formerly enlivened them had given way, momentarily at all events, to a distant coldness, with which he drew near to his guest.

"Herr Captain Almbach, you wish to speak to me?"

Hugo had already recovered from his astonishment, and resolved at once to take every advantage in his power of this unexpectedly favourable chance. He put forth all his capacities for pleasing.

"I am much obliged to you, sir. I hardly dared hope to be received personally by you."

Erlau sat down, and invited his guest by a sign to do the same.

"I am also medically advised to avoid visits, but at the mention of your name, I thought I ought to make an exception, as probably it concerns my guardianship of your nephew. You come on your brother's behalf?"

"On Reinhold's behalf?" repeated Hugo uncertainly, "How so?"

"I am glad that Herr Almbach has not attempted any personal intercourse, as he did once already in writing," continued the Consul, still in the same tone of cold restraint. "He appears, notwithstanding our intentional seclusion, to know of his son's presence here. I regret, however, being obliged to inform you, that Eleonore is not at all disposed--"

"Ella? Is she here? With you?" exclaimed Hugo so eagerly, that Erlau gazed at him in utter amazement.

"Did you not know it? Then Herr Captain Almbach, may I ask what has really caused me the honour of your visit?"

Hugo considered for a moment; he saw plainly that Reinhold's name, which had opened the doors for him, was nevertheless the worst recommendation which he could bring, and made his decision accordingly.

"I must first of all clear up a mistake," replied he, with thorough frankness. "I neither come as my brother's ambassador, which you seem to imagine, nor am I here, indeed, in his interest or with his knowledge. I give you my word for it, at this moment he has no suspicion that his wife and son are in the neighbourhood, or, still less, that they are even in Italy. I, on the contrary"--here the Captain thought it necessary to mix a little invention with the truth--"I on the contrary was put by chance on the track, and wished first of all to satisfy myself of its correctness; I came to see my sister-in-law."

"Which had better remain undone," said the Consul, with remarkable coldness. "You will comprehend that such a meeting could only be painful for Ella."

"Ella knows best how I have ever stood as regards the whole affair," interrupted Captain Almbach, "and she will certainly not refuse me the wished for interview."

"Then I do so in my adopted daughter's name," declared Erlau positively. Hugo rose--

"I know, Herr Consul Erlau, that you have gained a father's rights towards my nephew, and also his mother, and honour these rights. Therefore I entreat you to grant me this meeting. I will not wound my sister-in-law with one word, with one recollection, as you appear to dread, only--I should just like to see her."

Such a warm appeal lay in the words, that the Consul wavered; perhaps he remembered the time when young Captain Almbach's courage had saved his best ship, and how politely, but positively, he had rejected the gratitude which the rich merchant was ready to bestow so oppressively. It would have been more than thankless to have persisted in his sturdy refusal towards this man--he gave way.

"I will ask if Eleonore be inclined for this interview," he said rising; "she is already informed of your being here, as she was with me when I received your card. I must ask you to be patient for a few moments only."

He left the room. A short period of impatient waiting passed, when at last the door was again opened, and a lady's dress rustled on the threshold. Hugo went quickly towards the new comer.

"Ella! I knew you would not--" he stopped suddenly; his hand, stretched out in welcome, dropped slowly, and Captain Almbach stood as if rooted to the ground.

"You do not seem to recognise me quite," said the lady, waiting in vain for the rest of the greeting, "am I so much altered?"

"Yes, very much," said Hugo, whose glance still hung in intense astonishment on the figure of the lady before him. The impudent, confident sailor, who had hitherto always shown himself equal to every circumstance in his life, stood now dumb, confused, almost stupified. Who, indeed, could ever have deemed this possible!

This was what his brother's former wife had become, the shy, frightened Ella, with the pale unlovely face, and the awkward timid manner! Now only could one see how the dress had sinned, in which Eleanor Almbach always appeared like the maidservant, and never like the daughter of the house, and also that enormous cap, which, as if made for the brow of a person of sixty, had covered the youthful woman's head day after day. Every trace of all this had entirely disappeared. The light airy morning dress let the still girlishly, slight, delicate figure display itself in its full beauty, and the rich ornament of her fair plaits, which were now worn uncovered, encircled her head in all their heavy, glimmering, golden glory. Marchese Tortoni had not seen the face of the "blonde Signora," but Hugo saw it now, and during this contemplation of some seconds' duration, he asked himself, again and again, what had really taken place in these features, which were once so stolid and vacant that one reproached them with stupidity, and which now appeared so full of intellect and thought, as if a ban had been lifted from off them, and something, never suspected in them, awakened to life. Certainly around the mouth there lay a line of tender, unconquered pain, and her brow was shaded by a sadness it had formerly not known, but no more did her eyes seek the ground timidly, as if veiled; now they were clear and open, and they had truly forfeited none of their former beauty. Ella appeared to have learned not to hide any longer from the gaze of strangers that with which nature had endowed her. When she was eighteen, every one asked, shrugging his shoulders, "how does this wife come by that husband's side?" At eight and twenty, she was an apparition, fitted to compete with any one. How heavily must the burden and chains of her parents' house have rested upon the young wife, when only a few years in freer, nobler surroundings had sufficed to remove the former shroud, to the very last morsel, and to loose the wings of the butterfly. The almost incredible alteration proved of what her youthful education was guilty.

"You wished an interview with me, Herr Captain Almbach?" began Ella, as she seated herself upon an ottoman, "May I offer you a seat." Words and bearing were as assured and easy, as if coming from a perfect woman of the world receiving a visitor, but also distant and cool, as if she had no deeper concern in this visit. Hugo bowed, a slight colour tinged his cheeks, as he, following the invitation, sat down beside her.

"I begged for it. Herr Consul Erlau thought himself obliged to deny me this interview in your name, but I persisted in a direct appeal to you. I had more confidence in your goodness, my dear Madame."

She looked inquiringly with open eyes at him, "Are we become such strangers? Why do you give me this name?"

"Because I see that my visit here is considered as an intrusion to which I have no right, which I was not utterly denied, only on account of the name which I bear," replied Hugo, rather bitterly. "Herr Consul Erlau made me feel that already, and now I experience it a second time, and yet I can only repeat to you, that without the knowledge or on behalf of another, am I here, and that the other up to this moment has no suspicion of your vicinity."

"Then, I beg you to allow this vicinity to remain still a secret," said the young wife earnestly. "You will understand that I do not wish my presence to be betrayed, and S---- is far enough to make that possible!"

"Who told you that we are staying in S----?" asked Hugo, somewhat struck by the certainty of this conviction.

She pointed to some newspapers lying on the table--

"I read this morning that two of the greatest musical celebrities were expected there. The news has been delayed, as I see, and you are your brother's guest."

Hugo was silent; he had not courage to tell her how much nearer her husband was, and he could easily explain the notice in the papers to himself, as he knew of Beatrice's intended arrival. People were accustomed always to name her and Reinhold together, and although the latter was now even staying in Mirando, they considered his coming as certain, the moment she arrived in S----. Indeed it was also a pre-arranged meeting between the two, and could not be denied.

"But why this concealment?" asked he, leaving the dangerous point quite untouched. "It is not you, Ella, who have to avoid or flee from a possible meeting."

"No! but I will protect my boy at any cost from the possibility of such a meeting."

"With his father?" Hugo laid a reproachful stress upon the last word.

"With your brother--yes!"

Captain Almbach looked up surprised. The tone sounded freezingly cold, and a stony, icy look lay on the young wife's countenance, which all at once displayed the expression of an unbending will, such as no one would have expected in so pleasing an apparition.

"That is hard, Ella," said Hugo softly. "If you now render yourself unapproachable--I can understand it, after all that has happened; but why the boy also? Reinhold tried once already to communicate with his child; you repulsed him."

Ella interrupted him--

"You have told me that you come without any commission, Hugo, and I believe you; therefore this subject need not be discussed between us, let it rest! I was greatly astonished to see you again here, in Italy. Do you purpose remaining long?"

Captain Almbach took the hint given him, although somewhat taken aback by it. He was so unaccustomed for his young sister-in-law, whom he had almost always known as a silent, frightened listener, to govern the conversation so entirely, and lead it with such decision and ease to another topic when the former one had become painful to her.

"Most likely longer than I thought at first," said he, replying to her question. "My stay was originally only intended to be a short one, but a storm which caught us on the open sea, so dismantled the 'Ellida,' that I only reached the Italian harbour with great difficulty, and for the present cannot think of another voyage. The repairs will occupy some months, and my leave has therefore been prolonged indefinitely. I certainly never anticipated finding you here."

A shadow passed over the lady's face.

"We are here by medical advice," she replied sadly. "Weakness of his chest, obliged my adopted father to seek the south; his wife has been dead some years, and you know that he is childless. I had long since received all the privileges of a daughter, so that, of course, I also undertook the duties of one. The doctor insisted particularly upon this place, which indeed seems to exercise a most beneficial effect, and however much I might have desired to avoid Italy, I could not persuade myself to allow the invalid, to whom my presence is a necessity, to travel alone. We hoped to escape any painful meeting by avoiding the town in which Signor Rinaldo lives, and chose the most lonely, retired villa in order to obtain the greatest seclusion possible. Our precautions were in vain, as I see; you were no sooner in my vicinity than you discovered my whereabouts."

"I? Yes certainly," said Hugo with involuntary confusion. "And you reproach me with it."

Ella smiled.

"No, but I wondered that Herr Captain Hugo still entertained sufficient interest in the little cousin Ella, to insist so obstinately upon seeing her, when he was at first refused. We thought we had guarded amply against strange visits. You knew, nevertheless, how to force your entrance, and this shows me that I even possessed friends in my former life. Until to-day, I doubted it, but it is a fact which does me good, and I thank you for it, Hugo."

She raised her eyes clearly and openly to him; and with a charming smile, which made her face appear intensely lovely, she stretched out her hand to him. But the kindly thanks met with no response. Captain Almbach's brow burned deeply red, then he sprang up suddenly and pushed her hand aside.